Lucy Page

Lucy Page

A Cambridge Story of Love and Loss

Rosalind Seneca

Printed in the United States of America

Available from Amazon.com and other retailers.

ISBN-13: 978-1481282581
ISBN-10: 1481282581

Cover Photo: Kings College Chapel, Cambridge University, in winter.

Editing/Typesetting: Practical Pages, Green Brook, New Jersey

IN MEMORIAM

Lucy Page
1892–1972

Beloved piano teacher

About the Author

ROSALIND SENECA was born in Oxford, England, where she spent her early years. In 1963 she spent six months in Vienna before going on to Cambridge University, where she studied economics. In 1966 she traveled to America to attend graduate school, where she met her future husband, Joe. She made a career as a professor of economics, teaching at Drew University in Madison, New Jersey, where she now lives. She retired in 2004 and spends her time acting and writing. She and her husband have one son, who teaches high school English and drama and lives in Charlotte, North Carolina. *Lucy Page* is her first novel.

Contents

Contents

IV

Summer

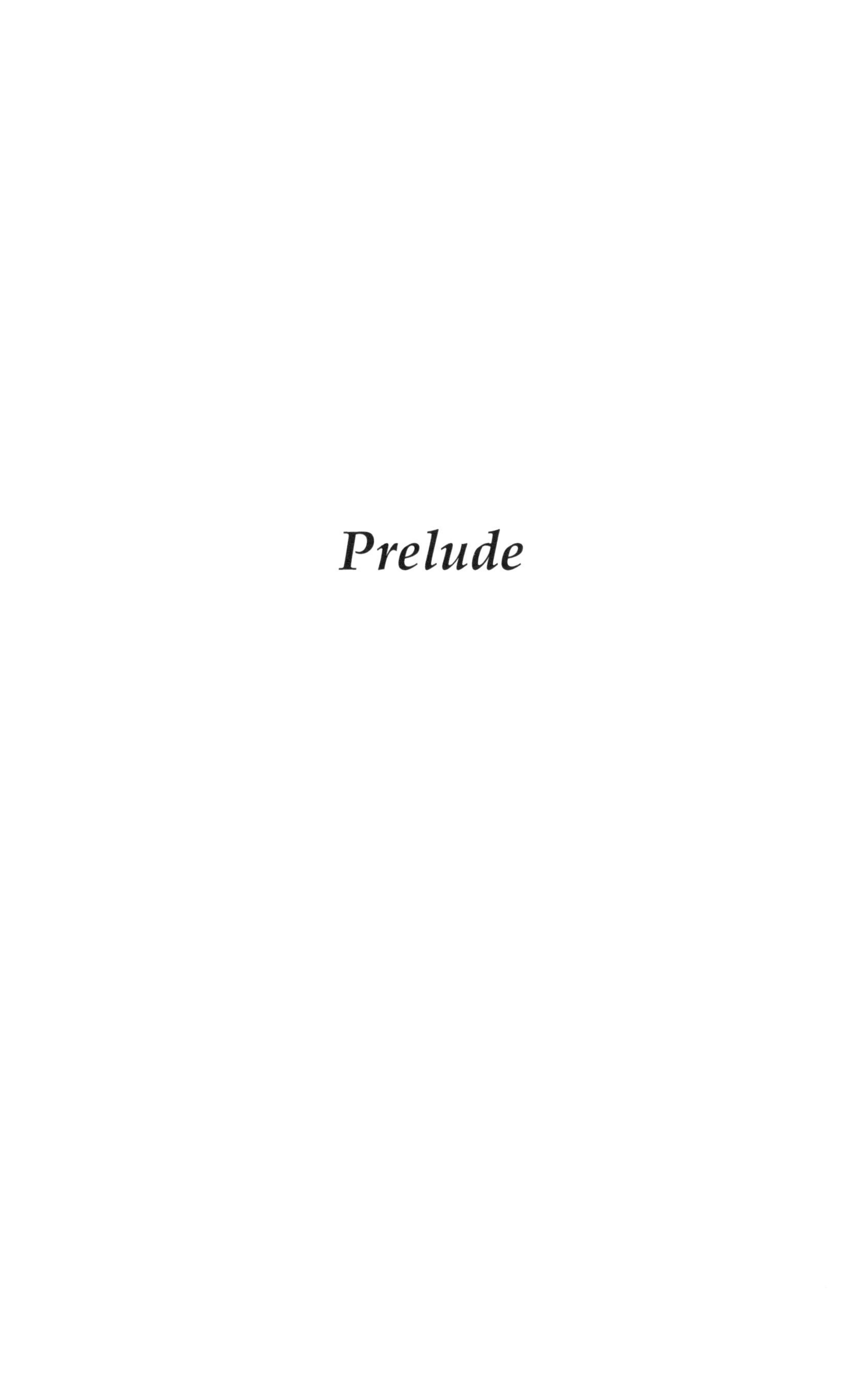

Prelude

Vienna

On a January day in 1963, Lucy Page was sitting in a train to Vienna and thinking about love. In particular, she hoped that she would soon fall in love and experience all the passion that she held inside her without incurring the depressing and inevitable judgment of her parents and her friends. So often they had rebuked her: "But Lucy, you're far too emotional; control yourself," when she expressed untrammeled enthusiasm or despair. Then she became angry, lost her temper, slammed the doors and shouted that no one understood her. But now she was free, nineteen years old, all on her own, and could imagine a grand passion without interference. She'd never been in love or even kissed, and she scarcely believed that any man would want to love her; but she still hoped.

They lived in London. Her father had taken her to the train at Victoria station and hugged her goodbye with an uncharacteristic warmth. She had felt a moment's pang at the parting but immediately turned her face toward the future. The ferry crossing to Ostend was at night and very cold, and she huddled in her bunk unable to sleep for excitement. She got up at dawn to see they were approaching the Belgian coast. When she disembarked at Ostend she was worried that she would not find the right train. But there it was, Number 119, waiting at the station with the notice "Express, Oostende-Wien" posted on every carriage. The compartment was luxurious, with wide red leather seats facing each other and a large window that was actually clean. Lucy had the window seat her father had carefully reserved.

Lucy adored traveling by train. She was reminded of the family holidays she had spent as a child in Scotland. The holidays began with an overnight train journey from London to Oban in the West Highlands. They slept on bunks, lulled by the comforting rocking of the train and woken on occasion by her father calling out the stations through which they passed: Crewe, Carlisle, Preston, Glasgow. She had loved these holidays. They had hiked among rugged mountains, jumping over little streams of clear water that pierced the bouncy green turf. The smooth surface of the cold, cold lochs had glimmered in the soft, slanting sunlight. A train journey was for Lucy the promise of something wonderful to come. Now the stations were all strange to her, but she counted them off in her mind in her father's voice, "Brussels, Koln, Frankfurt, Nurnberg, Linz" and finally, "Wien."

The carriage was almost full. On her right was an old lady with many suitcases and bags, wearing big boots. Lucy smiled at her and was acknowledged with an almost imperceptible nod. Opposite her was a young couple holding hands. Lucy was very interested but also embarrassed by this familiarity. She hadn't held anyone's hand since she was a child. Holding a man's hand in public seemed to her the height of intimacy. It showed mutual possession; it was an open sign of the secret world of love in which the couple dwelled. She longed for such a relationship. But now she looked away so as not to appear rude.

At lunch time the old lady reached into one of her bags and took out some dark bread, cheese, and salami, which she proceeded to eat with great relish. Lucy's family never ate salami—in fact, Lucy had not known what salami was until two girls at school whose parents were Russian had given a party and served precisely the kind of sandwich the old lady was currently enjoying. The old lady was probably German, though, because she got off the train at Cologne. Lucy looked at the timetable she had found on her seat. It was still many hours until Vienna, and she was impatient to arrive there.

Vienna had been the home of Lucy's piano teacher, Mrs. Clark. Mrs. Clark was an extraordinary person with a vibrant presence. She was rather stout with a lot of grey, curly hair and very tiny feet on which her body swayed gently as she talked and played. She had piercing black eyes and a mighty heart. When Lucy arrived for her lesson Mrs. Clark always embraced her as if she had been waiting for her all her life. Lucy greatly enjoyed her piano lessons and the concentrated attention that Mrs. Clark gave her. As well as a detailed instruction in technique, Mrs. Clark showed her how to give the music life. When, after weeks of technical work, she was allowed to play her Clementi sonatina or eventually a Beethoven sonata all the way through, Mrs. Clark would walk around the room listening and humming. Once, after she had played, Mrs. Clark burst out, "Oh Lucy, never, never lose this youth, this freshness." At such times Lucy felt her own soul rise up. She was inside the music, expressing it with her whole being, and she felt as if she were enfolded in Mrs. Clark's love and approval. After such a lesson she would feel so happy that she twirled her music case and sang her piano pieces as she skipped along the road to the bus stop.

Martha Clark, formerly Rosenstein, was born and brought up in Vienna. She had miraculously escaped the Nazis at the beginning of the war and, having lost all her family, had found herself in England teaching the piano to support herself. Lucy had never asked Mrs. Clark about her wartime experience; she learned her story only from a friend of her mother. She knew, however, that Mrs. Clark's particular method of teaching had been developed from that of her first husband. A picture of a handsome man with a wide mustache hung on the wall by the piano, and when Lucy asked her whether this was a picture of her father, she simply said "No," and Lucy inquired no further.

During her teen years Lucy had taken up the cello in addition to the piano, much to Mrs. Clark's dismay; she saw it as a distraction from the piano. Lucy's cello teacher was enthusiastic and kind and introduced Lucy to the joys of chamber music. But although Lucy loved her cello playing very much, she thought she was not as good a player as she wanted to be.

Lucy left school in December. She had stayed at school for an extra half-year after her A levels in order to study for the entrance exams for Oxford and Cambridge. To her great joy she was accepted by Cambridge and would begin her studies there the following October. She had chosen economics as her field. She thought she would like the subject and also thought it would please her father, who was an economist. There was a nine-month break to fill, and her fondness for Mrs. Clark drew her to Vienna, the home of Haydn, Mozart, Beethoven, and Schubert, and of so many things musical. Mrs. Clark was not encouraging. Vienna was the place in which she had lost everything to the Nazis, and she had never gone back there. But Lucy was determined. Her parents had generously agreed to support her there, a gift that she had taken for granted.

The farewell from her family had been easy for Lucy because she was so excited by the idea of seeing Vienna, but her mother had been very sad and worried.

"I'm going to miss you so much. I hope you'll find some friends," she said, incessantly tapping her fingers on her knee as she did when she was anxious. They had all been sitting round the brightly burning coal fire in the living room at home in London having tea. Even her father had come home early to join them because it was Lucy's last day.

"Make sure you find a good cello teacher," said her father, "though I don't suppose you'll ever play like Jacqueline du Pré." Lucy was unsurprised by her parents' remarks though she was hurt by her father's. She knew that what her father said was true, but she would much rather have had his encouragement and pride in her than this kind of truth. But she kept silent although vainly hoping for his praise.

"Of course, she'll meet friends," her older sister, Anthea, had said. "Look at me. I've been only one term at Oxford and I've found tons of friends. All you have to do is go to a few parties, and then invite people over for tea, and then they'll invite you back and before you know it you'll have a fantastic social life."

Anthea constantly talked about her life at Oxford, and Lucy was deeply jealous. Anthea had escaped the family for a whole term, and now she was back at home talking about all the people she had met, whom she liked and didn't like, the life at college with its parties and outings. But now Lucy felt warm even toward her sister.

She rejoiced in her freedom as the train sped on toward Vienna. There she would stay as a paying guest with a Viennese family called Mueller. She would take cello lessons in an attempt to find out if she could ever become a professional cellist. She did not think she could but she wanted to try. She turned her thoughts to the unknown. As she had watched the shores of England recede and with them her whole previous life, she had felt utterly alone, and relished the isolation. Now she could make whatever she wanted of her life. She had no friends in Vienna, so her new life was up to her; the uncertainty was exhilarating.

On the train Lucy spent most of the time looking out of the carriage window and drinking in the sights of the countries she passed through. She loved the little German villages, so neat and cared for amid the winter snow; piles of wood were exquisitely stacked by the cottages. "Everything in order," said the young man opposite her appreciatively. The train passed close to the great grey cathedral at Cologne, massive and looming. Then much later, as it came into western Austria, the spires of the churches were onion shaped—her first view of Baroque. They seemed the most romantic of all the buildings. Surely this new world would include a wonderful man with whom she could share everything. For Lucy, love would be the kind of intense romantic attraction that she had read about in the historical novels of Georgette Heyer; as the quiet, good heroine, she would fall in love with an extremely handsome and sophisticated man and suffer the pain of unrequited love until she finally discovered that her passion was shared. A beautiful but heartless competitor would be ousted and she, the heroine, would be married to the hero in a quiet, unassuming ceremony. At last she would be loved and appreciated.

These thoughts occupied Lucy's mind until the landscape became flatter and they approached Vienna and the Westbahnhof.

Lucy was met by Frau Mueller, a dumpy woman who wore a thick maroon coat and black fur hat. She had tied a white handkerchief around one arm as an agreed sign so that Lucy could recognize her. She gave Lucy a rather dour smile as she shook her hand and said "Welcome to Vienna" in a thick Austrian accent. She had virtually no other English, so Lucy was immediately forced to try out her German. But "Danke schoen" was all she managed to say. Frau Mueller had a car, and she drove Lucy through snow-covered streets between large ornamental buildings to a house in the suburbs of Vienna. The snow was piled high along the sides of the streets; Lucy had never seen so much. It was bitterly cold, and Lucy had no hat. Her wool winter coat was not proof against such cold. They drove into a small court in front of a fine large house. When they entered the house Lucy felt a rush of warm air. There were radiators in the hall; the house was centrally heated. Lucy had never once entered an English house or building during the winter without feeling a clammy cold that differed not one whit from the outside air; but this was pure luxury. Her room, upstairs and at the back, was large with windows looking out onto a big garden; the bed had no blankets but was covered with a spotless white duvet. A thick beige linen cloth was thrown over a large round table circled by four chairs. Lucy was entranced by a green wardrobe painted all over with colorful flowers and leaves. In this room there would be plenty of space to practice her cello. Frau Mueller left her alone to unpack and rest before having dinner.

When dinner time came, Lucy was introduced to the family, which consisted of Herr Doktor and Frau Mueller and two grown children, Hans and Elisabeth, both of whom lived at home. They seemed very well off, and Lucy could not quite understand why they needed her lodging payments to supplement their income.

"Come in, come in," said the Herr Doktor in a friendly tone, speaking in very slow German so that Lucy could understand. "Now let me see your glasses." Lucy was taken aback, but she duly took them off and passed them to him.

"You see," he explained, "I am an eye doctor, so naturally I want to see what kind of glasses you have. Ah, I see you are very short-sighted. Just let me know if you are not seeing well with these and I will get you another pair." Lucy did her best to thank him in her halting German. She hated her glasses because she was convinced that they stopped her from having any chance at being beautiful, even though she knew she was not. Her short, wavy brown hair and turned-up nose prevented that; the glasses were the last straw. And if she was not beautiful, what man would fall in love with her?

She sat down at the table and was shocked to find that the knives had swastikas on the handles. She was forced to consider whether the family had supported the Nazis during the war. Her young uncle, an RAF pilot, had been shot down by the Germans over the North Sea, and she felt guilty even picking up the knife. Could there be forgiveness? she wondered. It was all very unsettling.

"In England you have Shakespeare," said Doktor Mueller in a genial manner. "Do you remember Hamlet: 'To be or not to be?'" He proceeded to recite the entire speech in German; Lucy was most impressed. He continued his friendly talk throughout the meal and urged Lucy to play the piano in the living room whenever she liked.

In time Lucy discovered that Frau Mueller was always grumpy and hardly ever smiled. She spent a lot of time in the kitchen cooking the daily dinner. She made sure that Lucy had everything she needed but did not speak to her much or attempt to engage her in conversation. She would not allow Lucy to help with the dishes after dinner: "This is not your work," she said. Lucy, who had always helped with the dishes at home, felt both liberated and spurned. Lucy did not like her—she seemed to be a closed, inscrutable person.

A young maid from Yugoslavia lived with the family to help Frau Mueller. Her name sounded to Lucy like Jorjitsa; she never saw it written down. Poor Jorjitsa was thin, with lanky hair and a mottled complexion, and lived in a small room on the third floor. She had absolutely no English and very little German. Frau Mueller communicated with her using sign language and speaking in very loud, slow German. Jorjitsa did all the cleaning, dish washing, and laundry. When the sheets and duvet covers had been washed and dried Frau Mueller and Jorjitsa would seize opposite ends of a sheet and pull it to straighten it out before ironing. "Pull, Jorjitsa, pull," Frau Mueller would cry as they swayed at opposite ends of the room pulling away as if they were in a tug of war. Jorjitsa never ate with the family; she had her dinner alone in the kitchen. At home in England Lucy's mother had a charwoman; Mrs. Jones did the cleaning, washed the floors and the front door step, and talked a lot to Mrs. Page. The children were taught always to be friendly and polite to her, and since she was so much older than Lucy and lived elsewhere, Lucy had never thought of her as being, in fact, a servant. But Jorjitsa was Lucy's age, and Lucy was acutely aware of the difference in their status in the family. Was this so different from Mrs. Jones's position? she wondered. Lucy found herself extremely sympathetic to Jorjtisa and was frustrated that she had no way to express it. She recognized that Jorjitsa needed to earn her living but felt guilty that her own circumstances were so different. Compared with Jorjitsa she was like a little rich girl, even though her own family was not very well off.

The grown children were in their twenties. Hans was quite unlike his mother and would readily engage Lucy in conversation in excellent English. One day he told her that he had been present at the opening of the rebuilt Vienna Opera house ten years after the war.

"The opera was Fidelio," he said, "and you can imagine how we all felt while Beethoven's wonderful music about freedom was being sung."

"What freedom was Austria really celebrating?" she asked boldly. Hans looked at her suspiciously. "Why, from Germany," he snapped.

Lucy was most friendly with Elisabeth, whose room was next to hers. Sometimes Lucy had a different kind of fantasy about who she wanted to be other than the quiet, unsung Georgette Heyer heroine. In this second fantasy she dreamed of becoming a "femme fatale," a super-sophisticated, beautiful woman who would break men's hearts. Elisabeth was the embodiment of this fantasy. She was very tall and striking, with thick blond hair and grey-blue eyes. She had a very large, well-shaped mouth and a dead-straight nose. Her breasts were large and beautiful. Once when Lucy was with her in her room, Elisabeth changed her clothes to go out on a date. She stripped to the waist, exhibiting the fabulous swinging breasts, and put on a low-cut black dress with no bra underneath. This seemed to Lucy to be the height of daring. And indeed Elisabeth evidently enjoyed Lucy's shocked admiration. She would regale Lucy with stories of her suitors, old and young, and how she liked to flirt with men. Elisabeth was a cellist studying at the Akademie fuer Musik. She offered to introduce Lucy to Professor Pracht. "You must have my teacher," she said firmly.

Professor Pracht was a young, serious, and meticulous man with dark hair and eyes. His extremely dignified manner might have conveyed a sense of distance, had it not been for his great kindness and his sly sense of humor. He talked to Lucy in halting English (her German was not yet at all good) and seemed to like her. She played two notes for him and he stopped her.

"I will take you on," he said. "You must enroll in the Akademie as a beginner." Despite her tentative hopes, Lucy was not too shocked. She had been playing the cello for some years but she knew she was not a good player. She had heard Elisabeth play and recognized the great difference between them. He told Lucy he would teach her a good technique and would give her lessons twice a week on Mondays and Thursdays. He became Lucy's mentor as well as teacher. After she had finally been allowed to learn a "proper piece" as she called it, a sonata by Sammartini, Professor Pracht encouraged her as she played. "Singen Sie, Lucy, Singen Sie," he would cry, and Lucy felt she was playing like Rostropovich. He was in this respect like Mrs. Clark; he helped Lucy to find her soul and express it through the music.

Lucy also enrolled in a "German for Foreigners" course at the University that met twice a week. She practiced the cello every day and did her German homework very conscientiously. She soon began to make friends. At the class for foreigners she met a tiny, pretty Belgian woman, Therese, who was in Vienna to do a thesis on musical instruments. They quickly became close friends. There was also Jim, a jolly Englishman and Jorgos, a fat Greek whose concern for Lucy was palpable. He asked her where her parents were. "In England," Lucy replied, whereupon he asked her age. When Lucy said she was nineteen, he said, "but you look so young, I thought you were about twelve!" He made friendly attempts to improve her looks and told her that he didn't like the black wool hat she had bought to cover her unwashed hair. (In England, hair-washing was strictly once a week.) Lucy was not offended; she took each suggestion as it came, dumped the black hat, and washed her hair more frequently. She was reminded that she was very far from being the femme fatale of her fantasy.

At school Lucy had memorized the register of girls in her class. The register was taken every day and absences noted: Judith Adams, Ann Beecham, Lydia Cutslow. Lucy had sometimes thought, "I will remember this register for the rest of my life!" Her friends had been the same for her entire school life. But now she was able to choose her new friends as she liked. This was a heady experience. It was like sailing in uncharted waters. Therese was older than Lucy and seemed to her to be experienced and cosmopolitan, and Lucy tended to rely on her for sympathy and advice.

To begin with, Lucy went to concerts and the opera on her own. The first time she went to the opera she stood in a queue for three hours to obtain a standing-room-only ticket for *The Marriage of Figaro*. She was wearing her green Cambridge interview suit as she knew she should dress up but had nothing more suitable. The opera began and she found herself getting ever more tired in the standing crowd. All of a sudden, in the middle of Cherubino's famous aria, everything went blurry and she woke up outside in the corridor. She had fainted and been carried out. Her purse was handed to her and kind people were talking to her in German. She said in German, "I am English and I cannot understand German." An usher took her up to the top of the Opera house and gave her a seat where there was a blocked view of the stage. She could hear but not see the singers. She felt extremely disoriented. When she came home she looked up the word "to faint" in the dictionary, and next morning she said to Frau Mueller, "I fainted in the opera." Frau Mueller glanced up from her dishes and said with interest "Really, you fainted?" And Lucy, with some pride at being understood, said, "Yes, I did!"

Soon she was regularly accompanied by Therese. They would get cheap seats (no more standing) and sit in the balcony. Therese was twenty-three, an advanced age in Lucy's eyes. In fact, Lucy pitied Therese because she was not already married. And when Therese said, "Now that I'm twenty-three I can't rely on my looks any more and shall have to start using makeup regularly." Lucy silently agreed. Lucy herself used no makeup and would not have known how to begin to paint her face.

The Vienna of 1963 was a stately, stuffy, unhurried city. Lucy walked everywhere to see the sights. She admired the huge public buildings that stood along the Ringstrasse, each one built in a different style. She walked in the Volksgarten in the spring and relished the hundreds of roses. In Mozart's house in the Domgasse she felt personally connected to the great man. She fell in love with the spectacular jewels she saw in the crowns of the Hapsburg Emperors in the Treasure House at the Hofburg palace. One huge ruby drew her eye into its dark red liquid depths, and she coveted it. But like almost everywhere in Europe, Vienna was still shabby nearly twenty years after the end of the war, and seemed to Lucy to be very old-fashioned.

Lucy consumed concerts, operas, museums, churches, and the Austrian way of life. She filled herself with food. She ate dumplings stuffed with apricot jam, cheesecake, clear beef soup with large liver dumplings rolling around in the shallow bowl, sauerbraten with more dumplings, Wienerschnitzel, all kinds of little pastries exquisitely iced in different colors, and Sachertorte and Apfelstrudel with whipped cream. Her soul and body expanded together, and she was known to her friends as the "plump English girl." She bought a country Dirndlkleid, with a full flowered blue skirt, white bodice, and white lace apron, and noted with satisfaction that her breasts were larger. She felt a fullness she had never experienced before, and she was happy.

One day, the teacher of Lucy's German class, a tall beautiful woman called Ulla, invited the class to spend an evening in Grinzing at a Heuriger. The Heurige were old houses with large outdoor gardens festooned with hanging vines where the new wine was drunk. Long, friendly tables were set out, and everyone sat together on benches, friends and strangers alike. The wine was served in large glass beakers and tasted like lemonade; this was deceiving since it was very potent. Lucy went with Jim and Jorgos and was seated next to Ulla and opposite a young man called Gerhardt, an Austrian friend of Ulla's who seemed very jolly. He had bright blue eyes and fly-away brown, wavy hair. He looked at Lucy across the table and smiled. Lucy drank two beakers of wine and laughed and talked with Gerhardt in her still bad German.

"Do you like skiing?" she asked him. "I would love to go skiing. I have never done it before."

"Every Austrian skis," he replied. "There is always snow in the mountains in winter, and you can usually get there by train. We often go for several days, ski every day and spend the nights at a farmhouse or sometimes even in a hay loft."

"How wonderful," said Lucy. "In England it is always cold but there is rarely any snow. The winter is long and dark. How lovely that in Austria you can look forward to the winter as the time for excitement and beauty in the mountains!" This was a long speech for Lucy to make in German, and she managed it without too much help from Gerhardt. When she had finished she looked at him and laughed at herself. Gerhardt laughed with her and gazed into her green eyes.

"You must eat more bread and salami," he said, passing her a plate that the waiters had set between them. "It is good with the wine; it counteracts the effects of the alcohol."

So Lucy duly ate, but at the end of the evening still felt quite lightheaded. Gerhardt asked if he might walk her home.

They stepped out of the Heuriger into the calm, warm night. As they looked up at the moon and the stars shining in the infinite black firmament, Gerhardt took Lucy's hand. Lucy, who was swaying slightly from the wine, felt she was in heaven. Slowly they walked home, hand in hand and then, in a quiet street, Gerhardt turned Lucy toward him and kissed her lips. This was Lucy's first kiss. The softness and tenderness of it overwhelmed her. The feeling of intimacy was almost unbearable. She trembled, and her breath came in short gasps. They kissed again. "Your hair smells nice," he said. Lucy thought "hairspray."

"Only this moment," he said, and Lucy replied "of course." She didn't question the idea that this was just a fleeting encounter; it was too unexpected, too extraordinary to last, she thought. They had reached Lucy's house and kissed goodbye for the last time. She watched Gerhardt walking away up the street. She saw the back of his head and the way his hair moved in the wind. They never saw each other again.

The next day Lucy woke up with what she took to be the flu. She felt terribly sick and her head ached. She lay in bed all day nursing herself and cherishing the thoughts of the magical evening. Two days later, she described her sickness to Jorgos, who informed her that she had had a hangover!

July came, and Lucy returned to England in time to prepare for Cambridge. She knew now that she could never become a professional cellist and was looking forward to her studies in economics. She had had no grand passion in Vienna, but she thought constantly about her first kiss. She felt confident and happy and even felt that her family respected her more for having survived and indeed flourished alone in a strange country for seven months. She confided many of her experiences to her mother and sister; her father was interested only in her cello lessons and the musical events. She told no one about the kiss.

Part I

Michaelmas Term

1

Sarah's Circle

Michaelmas term began in Cambridge the first week of October. Lucy arrived at the station with all her luggage on a cold, rainy morning. The station was unimpressive and gave no hint of the beauties of the town, but on the taxi ride to Oldwick College she caught glimpses of them that she remembered from the time last year when she had come up for her scholarship interview. Cambridge was a quiet town, though it was filled with students during term. Its beauty lay in its college buildings and gardens, each college a gem. King's College Chapel was the diamond at the center on King's Parade, with its soaring spires and vast filigreed interior. Behind the chapel ran the small river Cam along which were ranged Clare, Caius, Trinity Hall, Trinity and St. John's Colleges. Each college had a bridge at the back that spanned the narrow river. The "Backs" of the colleges, seen from the river, were breathtaking; immaculate lawns came to the river's edge and trees spread their branches out over the slow moving Cam to form green arches. The town itself was built around the market square and Great St. Mary's church. In the open market, stalls sold fruit and vegetables and all sorts of delicacies. The male students would repair to a number of old pubs, and there were a few coffee shops and restaurants and a wonderful bookshop. But the centuries-old colleges dominated the town, with their fine chapels, libraries, and dining halls. Each college was its own little world, with the living quarters of the students and studies of the fellows surrounding pleasing courts. Oldwick College, one of only a handful of women's colleges, and a little way out of town, consisted of a series of large red-brick buildings joined by long, long corridors on three sides of well-kept gardens.

Lucy's room was at the top of Russell Hall, under the eaves. It was small but light and airy, with a view overlooking the gardens with their sunken lawns and herbaceous borders. Lucy put up some pictures of Vienna that she had bought from a street artist. She covered her bed with a red flowered bedspread that she and her mother had chosen together. She adored flowers and would have covered the white walls with floral paper if she could. There were a desk and two armchairs beside a gas fire which was fed with sixpences. On her first day, after she had finished unpacking, she sat on the window seat gazing first into her room and then at the view of the gardens and thought, "This is now my world and I am in it."

On the evening of the first day there was a freshman meeting for all the girls who lived in Russell Hall. It was led by the moral tutor whose role it was to act as a general adviser and counselor to the girls. She spent some time explaining the rules of the college: the times for meals, the rules of Hall, and so on. Finally, she noted that girls must be back in their rooms at 11:30 p.m. and that men could visit between the hours of 2:30 and 10:30 p.m. This all seemed eminently fair to Lucy, who had been brought up to be polite and obedient and to have a conservative view of behavior, although her politics, following her parents, were socialist. Lucy had met very few men during her school career and could not imagine inviting a man to her room—at least not yet. However, she did not quite see that restricting hours had much to do with morality since it was clear that the moral tutor did not monitor what went on in the rooms during the permitted hours. But, as usual, she asked no questions.

On the afternoon of her second day at Oldwick, Lucy knocked on the door of the room next to hers. The name on the door was Sarah Hardy, and Lucy bravely decided to introduce herself. Sarah called out a soft "Come in," and Lucy entered a most surprising room. It was small, like Lucy's, and the window also looked out on the gardens. But unlike Lucy's room it was dark and mysterious. Light coming through thin red cotton curtains partially drawn across the windows cast a red glow in the room. Indian bedspreads in dark green and blue with beige patterns on them hung on the walls with another arranged on the bed. On the floor was a threadbare oriental rug, also red. The desk was covered with papers, and books were everywhere. In a space on the wall not covered by bedspreads was a reproduction of a painting by Matisse of women dancing in a circle. Lucy had not seen it before and looked at its fluid and exuberant lines with interest. The gas fire glowed, and Sarah sat on one of the two armchairs beside it.

Lucy introduced herself tentatively. "Do come in and sit down," said Sarah, putting down a book and waving Lucy to the other armchair. Sarah looked just like her room. She wore a long black skirt rolled up a bit at the waist, apparently to prevent it from dragging on the ground, and a loose green cotton blouse under a very large grey woolen cardigan. On her head she had tied a green silk scarf beneath which straggly black locks fell to her shoulders. Lucy thought of Jorgos and his hair-washing lecture. She wore clog-like shoes on her feet, and Lucy wondered how she rode her bike in them. Her face was long and thin with dark, glowing eyes and a thin mouth. When she smiled her face lit up like a pixie. She was smoking a cigarette as she was reading.

"I've just come up, and I'm feeling rather overwhelmed," said Lucy. "There are so many things to find out about and so many rules to learn. I'm even intimidated by dinner in hall."

"Oh, you'll get used to it," said Sarah with a supercilious air, waving her cigarette hand vaguely. "Everyone does. When I first came up last year I didn't realize that you had to be absolutely on time for dinner and that if you were late you had to bow to the Principal on High Table as you entered the room. I really don't like following rules, but here you are somehow drawn into the way of things. Everyone takes the rules so seriously. In fact, in Cambridge everyone takes everything so seriously you would think that Cambridge was the center of the world."

"Oh, that's how it is," said Lucy, relieved that Sarah had explained things so clearly. "What's your subject?"

"English," replied Sarah, "Especially women writers, I love the nineteenth century. What are you reading?"

"Economics," said Lucy. "I don't know much about it yet, but it's my father's subject, and he seems to find it interesting."

"Very brave of you to do your father's subject, especially such a difficult one," said Sarah.

"Oh, do you think so?" asked Lucy, slightly worried. "I hadn't quite thought if it that way. In fact, Lucy thought a lot about her father, who was very brilliant. She was intellectually able and had always done well at school, but no matter how well she did she could not gain the approval of her father, who would always set the bar higher. However, she kept trying. She loved him but seemed unable to connect with him.

"What book are you reading?" she asked Sarah.

"Bronte's *Shirley*," replied Sarah. "It's got some extraordinary passages about the horrible position of women in society. Listen to this:

> What do fathers expect their daughters to do at home? If you ask, they would answer, sew and cook. They expect them to do this, and this only, contentedly, regularly, uncomplainingly all their lives long, as if they had no germs of faculties for anything else. . . . Could men live so themselves? Would they not be very weary? And, when there is no relief to their weariness, but only reproaches at its slightest manifestation, would not their weariness ferment in time to phrenzy?

Sarah explained, "That's spoken by Caroline, who is a spinster living at home with her cold uncle. She is gentle and retiring. But she wants to go and work as a governess, earn her own money, and have something worthwhile to do during the day to replace the unutterable uselessness she feels as a poor dependent."

Lucy was taken aback by this little lecture. She had hardly entered the room and now she was being asked to think about the position of women in society. Sarah was so absorbed by what she had just said that she didn't seem to notice Lucy at all. There was silence. Finally Lucy said, "Aren't we lucky that we can come to Oldwick and use our brains!"

"Oh yes," said Sarah, "But then everyone will go off and get married and be enslaved again."

"Is marriage really so undesirable?" asked Lucy. "I'm rather looking forward to it." Lucy could not imagine herself capable of doing anything much except to be a good student, and marriage was her ultimate goal in life. She had not much idea of a career and thought only vaguely about going into the civil service or teaching.

"Marriage is a state of oppression for women," said Sarah "Women do all the housework, care for the children, and lose their minds."

Lucy thought of her own mother, endlessly making beds, doing laundry, and cooking meals while trying to fit in a part-time teaching job. Her father did no housework at all. But her mother seemed sane; always worried, but definitely sane. Could marriage really drive you mad?

"But don't you want to be married?" asked Lucy, now reconciled to the serious tone of the conversation.

"Of course not," said Sarah, "I'm enjoying my independence from my parents at home. The last thing I want is to depend on a man. That is not going to be my lot. I'm not going to waste my education. I am going to work for women and help to teach them that there are possibilities for a life path other than getting married."

"Well, I see what you mean," said Lucy. "It is wonderful to be alone and to be able to decide what to do each day without having to take anyone else into account."

"Yes, it is," agreed Sarah.

"You seem to have your ideas very well worked out," ventured Lucy. "I change my mind about how I think about things every second. How long have you been thinking about all this?"

For a moment Sarah lost her assured air and looked slightly sheepish. "Oh, I had a friend at school who was a feminist," she said lighting up another cigarette. She got up and walked to the window where she drew the curtain back and looked out. "She explained to me about the patriarchy."

Lucy felt out of her depth, but she really wanted to understand Sarah, so she used an annoying technique of her father's and instead of asking what the patriarchy was, thereby revealing her ignorance, she adopted his professorial air and asked, "What exactly do you mean by the patriarchy?"

"Oh, Lucy," replied Sarah impatiently, "You know, it's the whole set of institutions in society that are set up to privilege men and oppress women. You'll have to come to my Circle where we talk about such things. Do come, we meet on Thursday afternoons. And then you'll meet all my friends."

Lucy did not think she had much to contribute about the patriarchy, but it would be nice to meet the other women, so she said, "Thanks so much, I'd love to come." As she left Sarah's room her mind was full of the idea that marriage and independence did not go together.

Lucy met Sarah's Circle when she went to their next meeting. Although she was a socialist like her parents, her views about the appropriate relationship between men and women were quite conventional, and she did not know what to expect. The group met in Charlotte Bradley's room in Bainton Hall, which was large and full of sunlight streaming in through two sets of windows. In spite of the sun, the room was cold, being heated only by a small gas fire at one end. Lucy was welcomed by Charlotte herself. Sarah was sitting on the floor by the fire in true college custom. Charlotte was very glamorous, with long, straight black hair that fell over her face when she turned or looked down. When she started to talk she flicked her hair back to reveal beautiful dark eyes, red cheeks, and a full mouth with a trace of soft dark hair on the upper lip. She wore a black ruffled sweater and grey pleated skirt. A big white silk scarf with a bright blue and red border was cleverly tied to display one huge red flower. The elegant scarf set her apart from the other girls at Oldwick that Lucy had met so far. Like Lucy, they all wore the "Oldwick uniform" which also consisted of a jumper and skirt, but Charlotte's appearance was positively chic. She had an exaggerated way of speaking with emphasis, and she was open and friendly to Lucy. "Oh, DO come in and DO sit down next to me," she said, "we're toasting the most FANTASTIC crumpets, you simply HAVE to taste one." Lucy took the offered crumpet, buttered it, and let her teeth sink into it with relish. Feeling reassured, she looked around the room.

"I'm so glad you came," Charlotte said. "Everyone's dying to meet you."

"Yes," said Sarah, "we're all such literary types we need a good dose of practicality."

"I don't know whether economics is exactly practical, but it's certainly about nuts and bolts and guns and butter," said Lucy, quoting from her first lecture.

"Good heavens, I'd much rather read a novel," said Charlotte.

Now another woman whom Lucy recognized came in; she had spoken to her before at dinner and found out that her name was Hannah. She was a very large person who wore, like Sarah, a long dark skirt and a colorful patchwork jacket. Her long, thin brown hair was taken back into a ponytail and fastened with a rubber band. She had a plain but very intelligent, mobile face. She sat down in an arm chair, took out some knitting, and began to unroll her wool. She was evidently making a large green jumper. She looked at Lucy when she was introduced and said, laughing, "I know, you weren't expecting a so-called emancipated woman to knit, were you? I knit because I like the feeling of creating something while we talk, and besides, I find it soothing. This jumper is for my boyfriend, Max." Lucy found it odd that Hannah had mentioned him immediately at a women's circle. Never having had a boyfriend, Lucy was longing to know about their relationship and whether they were truly in love, but she suppressed her desire to ask about it directly. She turned to Sarah, who was offering her a cup of tea.

"Hannah's doing what Charlotte Bronte says will drive women into a frenzy," said Sarah smugly. Hannah sent an amused, tolerant smile in Lucy's direction. Lucy had no idea whether anyone was being serious.

Last to come in was a short, dumpy girl with a sad face and a frown that made her seem as if she disapproved of the whole world and everyone in it. Her mouth turned down, and she seemed to avoid looking directly at anyone in the room. Her hair, though, was beautiful—a reddish-brown color, very long, thick and curly. Her fingernails were bitten to the quick. She wore a very neat, old-fashioned dress cinched at the waist with a belt of the same fabric and big lace-up shoes.

"This is Anne," said Sarah. Anne managed a brief hello and immediately placed herself next to Sarah on the floor. Sarah was looking confident and cheerful, and sent a bright smile toward Lucy. "We have a topic for each meeting," she said, "and today the topic is self-doubt."

Charlotte flicked her hair back. "Well, I can't imagine why you picked this topic, it's ridiculous. I never doubt myself. I try hard every day to do the right thing, and when I go to bed at night I say to myself, 'Jolly good, old girl, well done.' I simply don't see the point of self-recrimination." Silence followed this remark as if this statement by Charlotte had dealt with the topic completely. Lucy found Charlotte's comment very reassuring. What was there to say about this topic after all? The fire hissed gently, and outside the window the sun shone low in the sky, casting long shadows in the room. Then, surprisingly, Anne looked at Sarah as if to gather confidence, and spoke to Charlotte:

"How can you not doubt yourself, Charlotte? I doubt myself all the time."

"Well, why, Anne?" said Charlotte.

"Oh, I don't know," said Anne reluctantly, "something about my childhood, I suppose."

"Oh, so you're a victim of your parents, are you?" said Charlotte, shaking her head with a sigh.

"Come on, Anne," said Sarah comfortingly "you can tell us."

"I'd really rather not," said Anne. "I can't imagine that you would be interested in my difficulties with my mother. Charlotte's right; everyone blames their parents, and it gets so boring." Boring was the ultimate pejorative word. The worst thing you could say about a person was that she was boring.

Hannah paused in her knitting, pulling out some more wool, and said, "I think Anne's got a right to keep her experience to herself if she wants. You can't demand that people tell you their thoughts, Sarah."

Anne became flustered at the argument she seemed to have caused. "No, it's all right," she said, "it's just that when I was a child, for instance, my mother used to cross-question me about what had happened at school every day. If I said I had been ignored by the other girls, my mother would deny it and say 'Of course you weren't, you were just being shy; you should be friendlier and then the other girls will like you.' Or if I said the art mistress liked my painting, she would say, 'Well, I'm sure she liked all the other paintings too, you really mustn't boast.' So I would begin to doubt myself and my own reactions, and then I simply wouldn't tell her about anything because I didn't know whether what I had experienced had really happened in that way. And I still don't know where I stand with anyone or anything."

Sarah said hastily, "But surely you know where you stand with us, don't you, because we are all friends here who are honest with each other."

"I suppose so," said Anne as she sipped her tea reflectively, "But I just don't see how Charlotte can be so sure of herself; I think she's denying her self-doubt."

"I am not," said Charlotte crossly. She got up, put a few more sixpences in the fire slot, and started to roam around the room, waving her arms as she spoke. "I just don't see the point of worrying about myself all the time; I just forge ahead. My mother was hopeless too and always worrying about things like whether we were in time for the bus, or what we should have for dinner, or whether I was doing my homework well enough; it bothered me until I was about twelve, and then I understood that it was just how she was and refused to be affected by it. So I knew I was on my own and said to myself, 'You're all right.'"

Lucy was full of admiration. Hannah looked up from her knitting and said, "But it's all really a matter of faith. The question is how to have faith in oneself, and I don't think you can unless the faith comes from God. Surely our inner security comes from the faith that God loves us, and that we love God and it is that spiritual bond which gives us the wherewithal to do our lives."

The group looked as startled as if a bomb had gone off. Sarah said, "Oh Hannah, for goodness sake. I'm the daughter of religious parents and I don't bring God into everything. I just think people ought to be left alone to believe what they like."

Lucy found herself in some conflict as she listened to the discussion. She often felt like Anne, but she was also drawn to Hannah's solution to self-doubt. Lucy's mother had taken her to church and Sunday school, which she loved. But she had waited and waited for God to speak to her. He never did, not even when she was confirmed. So she had given up and concluded that God didn't exist for her. But Hannah's words had brought all her spiritual yearning flooding back. Surely it was right that God in us was the source of all security.

"You're all missing the point," Sarah went on. "The real point is that women have been taught self-doubt by men. The patriarchal system teaches us to view ourselves as inferior, cuts us off from education and jobs, and teaches us that all we can do is sew and cook."

"Nonsense," Charlotte said, "look at us, we're all getting a fine education, and I for one plan to get a job as a journalist when I graduate. I refuse to admit that I'm a victim in any way. That's a terrible trap. It means it's all right to blame someone else for your own difficulties. I don't think either my parents or men in general have that much power over me."

Anne looked away as if she were ashamed, and Lucy was also brought up sharp by this outburst. She was deeply interested in and attracted to men and did not see this as a symptom of exploitation. On the contrary, she thought that a loving relationship with a man would be the most sustaining experience of her life. So far she had not spoken a word in the whole discussion. But suddenly she found herself saying, "Don't we find our inner security in a relationship with another person?" There was a brief silence. Everyone sipped on the cold tea at the bottom of their cups and looked perplexed.

"What do you mean, Lucy?" asked Anne, looking up at her and losing her frown.

"Well, for instance, I've had two fantastic music teachers and I had what I think is a wonderful relationship with both of them. Every time I was with them I learned so much, both about music and also about how one should live one's life. I felt they understood me, and they gave me inner security."

"So they were like surrogate parents," observed Anne.

"Well, I suppose so," acknowledged Lucy, "I certainly loved them like parents. But the point is that they weren't my parents." This statement was now followed by a lot of talking as Sarah and Charlotte tried to make their points over again. They were all talking together and then began to laugh; Lucy found that she was caught up in the moment and started to laugh herself. More tea was poured and crumpets toasted and the whole atmosphere became very convivial. When the tea was finally over and Lucy was walking back to her own room she concluded that she had had a very stimulating time.

The next day, Lucy was working at her desk when Anne came to her room. "I do hope I'm not disturbing you," said Anne, whose frown reflected her tentative tone of voice. "I just came up to see you because I liked what you said yesterday and wondered if you had enjoyed the meeting with the group."

"Oh, I am glad you came, Anne," said Lucy cheerfully, "do come in. Now I have a proper excuse for taking a break."

Anne looked around the room with interest. She immediately admired the pictures of Vienna and asked Lucy about her stay there.

"What are the Austrians like now?" she asked. "Weren't they all Nazis during the war? Are they still Nazis?" Lucy felt suddenly quite defensive and was about to give a short negative response when she thought about Doktor and Frau Mueller and the swastikas, and then about Mrs. Clarke, and realized that, if there was a true answer, it was certainly very complicated. So she replied calmly, "I'm not very good on the history of Austria. But I love the Austrians now because they seem so free, so prepared to examine the true nature of human beings, so deep. Not like the English way of denying the emotions and saying 'Well, just get on with it' to everything. Most of the people I met in Austria were friendly and helpful. And I loved the music above all. You just haven't really heard what a waltz sounds like until you've heard the Viennese play it."

"Oh," said Anne, "I see," standing rather awkwardly in front of the fire.

"Look," said Lucy, "why don't you stay and have a glass of sherry with me."

"I'm afraid I don't drink," said Anne, blushing with embarrassment. The conversation was not going well. Lucy was silent but Anne, looking at Lucy's cello propped up against a chair, tried again.

"Are you going to play your cello in Cambridge?" she asked.

"I hope so," replied Lucy, "I'm certainly going to try to get into the University Orchestra and maybe find some chamber music too. Do you play an instrument?"

"I wish I did," replied Anne. "But I have a friend in the orchestra who plays the flute, so I always go to the concerts; they're awfully good."

Lucy looked at Anne and thought what a contrast she was. On one hand she seemed very shy and easily embarrassed; on the other hand, when she did speak, she said exactly what she thought and was quite open about her thoughts, far more open than Lucy was prepared to be. Lucy would never have discussed her difficulties with her father as openly as Anne had discussed her mother yesterday at the Circle. She said, "Well, I hope when you next come to hear your friend play you'll also be hearing me too."

Silence fell once again, and they both found themselves looking out of the window. Lucy said, "What kinds of things do you like to do, Anne?"

"Photography," she replied immediately. "I joined the photography society last year and I've learned so much. I can develop and print my own photographs now." Lucy was impressed and said so. The atmosphere in the room began to warm up, and very soon she and Anne were talking amicably together. Their conversation seemed to erase Lucy's initial confusion about Anne; her shyness, and at the same time her forthrightness, were evidently different sides of a very interesting girl. As they went downstairs to dinner, Lucy felt she had found a friend.

2

Adam

Lucy was in the habit of checking her post three times a day. The postboxes were next to the Porter's lodge on the way out of the college. Post from other colleges was delivered twice a day and anyone inside the college who wanted to make contact could simply drop her a note. Receiving post was very exciting, every letter holding the promise of something new.

One day, about a month into Michaelmas term, she found a note from an Oldwick student who lived in Darwin Hall. It read,

> *Dear Lucy,*
>
> *Would you like to come to tea on Thursday at 4:00? I have a friend, Adam Wagner, from Vienna who says he knows you and would like to meet you again. It would be very nice if you could come. My room is Darwin 26.*
>
> *Yours sincerely, Fiona Banks*

Lucy was mystified. She did not know Fiona and she had certainly never met a man called Adam in Vienna. She thought about her friends there but could not conjure up any connection. It was all very mysterious, and she almost allowed herself to think that she had a secret admirer (she still held onto her fantasy of being a femme fatale). The promise of meeting him was a magnet, and so on Thursday she climbed the stairs in Darwin Hall to number 26. A woman flung the door open and said in a very gushy voice, "Oh you must be Lucy . . . oh, do come in, and find a seat and do have some tea."

Fiona was very pretty. She had a perfect eighteenth-century face with bright blue eyes and masses of thick, curly blond hair. She had full breasts that she carried before her like a ship's figurehead. She sported very high heels so that her bottom stuck out behind her in an inviting sort of way. She wore a silk blouse with one too many buttons undone and a stylish pleated skirt. Lucy looked at her and felt distinctly shabby.

The small room was cozy; covering the white walls were interesting pictures and photographs including a big poster with "Braque" written in large letters across the bottom. Lucy had never heard of Braque and was impressed. The bed had a white duvet on it that reminded Lucy immediately of Austria. The gas fire was turned on full, with a pile of sixpences next to it to ensure a continuous glow. The room was crowded; a number of girls and two men were seated on chairs, on the floor in front of the fire, and on the window seat, all talking animatedly. Lucy knew no one, but she sat down on the floor by the fire and was introduced to two of the girls, Jane and Camilla. They were talking about their director of studies.

"She's such an odd woman," said Jane. "She dresses appallingly and is always fondling her old cat so that the hair gets all over the front of her jumper. And she offers us sherry, but the glasses are positively greasy; I mean, how can sherry glasses get greasy?"

"I know exactly what you mean," said Camilla. "I hardly dare to sit on a chair in her room because everything is so grubby."

"But she is interesting," conceded Jane, "so I suppose we shouldn't mind about the ghastly jumper."

Lucy looked down at her own jumper. It was a nice soft green. At least there were no cat hair or stains, but she noted that Jane and Camilla were wearing rather fetching blouses like Fiona. Lucy had very few clothes and certainly no silk blouse. Her mother had no interest in clothes, and her own sense of style was quite undeveloped. She pulled at her silver pendant, patted her hair to reassure herself, accepted a mug of tea from Fiona, and started to toast a piece of bread on a toasting fork in front of the fire.

"Phoebe is going to try out for the Dramatic Society's production of *As You Like It*," continued Jane. "Of course, she wants Rosalind, but I frankly don't think she's up to it. She's just so serious, and Rosalind should be light and funny."

"I know what you mean," replied Camilla. "She doesn't seem to have the flair. But of course one can't say anything discouraging. You just have to tell her you hope she gets the part, even though you know it's unlikely and she'll be dreadfully disappointed when she doesn't."

"On the other hand," said Jane, "she does seem to be rather thick with that smarmy chap who's directing it. The one who smokes a lot and is always lording it around as if he's Laurence Olivier."

"Yes," said Camilla with a disappointed laugh, "so she might get it after all. It's always who you know."

Lucy hated the tone of the gossip and began to feel like sticking up for the unknown Phoebe. At that moment she saw Fiona stumble with the tea pot and spill some tea on Camilla's skirt. Without any apology, Fiona said in her gushy voice, "Oh dear, never mind, well, just get it cleaned and send me the bill, just send me the bill." Camilla looked annoyed but said nothing, and wiped her skirt vaguely with a handkerchief.

Lucy was beginning to wonder about Adam. Her heart sank. It was already half past four and he had not arrived. Maybe he wasn't coming. Or perhaps he didn't know that one was supposed to be punctual, and he was just fashionably late. She realized that she was dying to meet him.

At last there was a soft knock on the door; it opened; a beautiful male face peered round it and scanned the room. Lucy stared at this face with its angular jaw and its smooth and slightly dark complexion. The eyes were brown and liquid with extremely long lashes and beautifully shaped eyebrows, and the generous, full mouth showed at first just the hint of a smile. The dark, straight hair had been combed just so. This aristocratic foreign face transported Lucy back to the cafes and concerts in Vienna where she had observed the men drinking coffee so comfortably or escorting their wives with an air of tremendous self-confidence as they greeted other people and kissed the hands of the ladies, all the while looking into their eyes. Now the face smiled a beautiful smile, a questioning smile, a smile that asked, "Is there anyone interesting here? Should I come in?" Before the door had opened further and the whole person had entered the room, Lucy had fallen in love.

The man lived up to his face. He had a slim figure and was impeccably dressed. He was wearing a well-cut, dark tweed jacket and brown tie, and his shoes were brightly polished. Lucy glanced at the shoes of the other two men in the room. By comparison they looked positively scruffy. Lucy pulled at her hair nervously as Fiona rushed to the door and took the man familiarly by the arm.

"Here you are at last, Adam," she cried. "We've all been waiting ages for you. Come and see Lucy."

Lucy thought Adam looked a bit surprised and instantly wondered if he had been expecting a more beautiful girl. She had not worn her one nice dress, thinking that it would seem too posh for tea. So at first she looked at him rather nervously, but as soon as he approached her she began to smile her best lively, welcoming smile.

Adam came and sat on a chair right next to her as she toasted her bread. He looked at her directly with a flattering interest. His voice was deep and softly accented. His English was perfect.

"What are you reading?" he asked.

"Economics," replied Lucy, "My tutor is Miss Mead."

"I know who she is," said Adam, "a plain woman with very large legs."

"Oh, but she's so nice," said Lucy leaping to her defense. "What are you reading?"

"I'm doing an M. Phil in Economics, so we have that in common."

"Oh, have you been to Professor Hill's lectures? He's very clear." She stopped while she searched for something more interesting to say. Then she said boldly, and inspired by the conversation in Sarah's Circle, "Have you noticed that when Professor Hill talks about his model of consumer behavior, he calls the two consumers Mrs. A and Mrs. B, but when he talks about the two entrepreneurs, he calls them Mr. C and Mr. D?"

"Well, of course," laughed Adam, "that's the way it is and that's the way it should be."

"I don't agree at all," she said. "Surely men can be consumers and women can be managers." Lucy had surprised herself; she was trying to flirt but instead she was saying provocative things to a man she had only just met.

"Don't you think women should manage their own homes?" asked Adam.

"Well, of course," she replied, "managing a home requires intelligence and skill, and it's very hard work, but surely they could also manage firms."

Adam looked at her curiously. He took the piece of toast she offered him, buttered it, and spread it lavishly with strawberry jam. Then he changed the subject and asked, "What is your essay topic for this week?"

"Marginal Utility," replied Lucy. "How do you say that in German?"

He told her with a half smile that made her feel her ignorance. Finally, she asked, "How do you know me? We certainly did not meet in Vienna."

"We both know Otto; I was his student at the university," he said.

Otto was a friend of Ulla's whom Lucy had once met when she was visiting Ulla. Otto taught at the university and had evidently taught Adam there. But she hardly knew Otto, so she could not imagine what kind of description he must have given Adam to interest him enough to want to look her up. And why had Adam said to Fiona that he knew her already? It seemed so unnecessary to lie. Lucy was momentarily put off, but Adam, looking slightly embarrassed, quickly said, "Did you like your stay in Vienna?"

Lucy found herself becoming extremely animated. She looked at this handsome Viennese man and forgave him the lie. She talked a great deal about her experiences in Vienna, her cello teacher, and the concerts she had attended.

"I heard Karajan conduct Beethoven's 'Symphony No. 9,'" she said. "I wonder why I find Beethoven so consoling. He makes me cry in the slow movement, but then in the final 'Ode to Joy' I get so filled up with happiness that I feel like running through walls."

Adam replied, "Ah, I can see you love passionate music."

"Yes," she said, "I suppose I do. I love the outpouring of music, the wonderful melodies, and the sweeping scale. I'm afraid I don't get on with twentieth-century music at all, especially not Bartok!"

"But such wonderful rhythms," said Adam.

Lucy was silent, She was afraid she had been revealing too much about herself. But Adam laughed and responded with stories about his family and particularly about his younger brother—his "little" brother, he called him—with whom he was very close.

"As children we were always together," he said. "We would tell each other everything. We played chess together, and I always won. He accepted it; he knew I had to win! And now that we are grown up we are still the best of friends."

"Are you still winning?" asked Lucy.

"In most things, yes, but not in tennis. There I let him beat me."

"I was close to my sister," said Lucy, "but not so much now. When we were little children we always played together. We each had seven dolls and our game was called 'Mrs. Brown and Mrs. Jones.' Our husbands were always out at work, and we dressed our dolls and took them out for walks, gave them tea from tiny tea cups, and then put them to bed and read to them. It was a wonderful game that lasted till I was about 11 years old. After that we drew apart. I was always jealous of Anthea because she did everything first since she was the oldest. It is so nice that you and your brother are so close."

Adam said nothing but looked at Lucy and smiled his beautiful smile. Already, only minutes after his entry into the room, Lucy was under Adam's spell. Her heart and soul opened and took in this beautiful Austrian man with his soft voice and teasing manner. He was a complete mystery to her and yet she loved him. It seemed a very natural thing. He appeared to have all the qualities she was searching for, everything she had imagined in her fantasies. But how could this fabulous man possibly like her? Her appetite for the toast and tea deserted her; she felt slightly sick, and she had butterflies in her stomach.

The bell for dinner rang and the group broke up. Adam said vaguely that he hoped he would see her again. Lucy ran back to her room for her gown. Her heart sang. As she came back out of her room she ran into Sarah, who took one look at Lucy's flushed face and cried, "My God, what's happened to you, you look radiant!"

Lucy's voice, low and breathy, came from somewhere deep inside her. She said, "I've met a man."

LLL

Three days went by, and Lucy lived alternately in a state of glorious expectation and restless uncertainty. She thought about Adam constantly—as she bicycled to her lectures through the streets thronged with students, as she sat in the library hoping to catch a glimpse of him, and as she sat on the floor in her room by the fire, toasting a crumpet and hoping for a knock on the door. She avoided Sarah and was grateful that the Circle was not meeting again until the next week. She did not want her experience of meeting Adam to be belittled.

On the third day she picked up a note written in tiny handwriting.

Dear Lucy,

It would be very nice if you would come out to dinner with me on Saturday. We could go to the Garden House restaurant. Could I pick you up at 7:00?

Yours sincerely, Adam Wagner

The magic door had opened and Lucy stepped through it into a transformed world, a green and sparkling meadow filled with summer flowers blooming, buttercups, poppies, daisies, irises, and sunlight streaming so brightly she could not see where the meadow led. She was now beautiful; she put her hand to her shining hair and felt her body straighten and relax as if she were floating. She ran back to her room to her desk and wrote a quick note of acceptance. Now she could wear her red fitted dress with its black turtleneck collar and her gold necklace. She might even put her hair up into a chignon if she could make it stay.

She was ready by 6:30 on Saturday and spent the next half-hour pacing her room, waiting. At precisely seven o'clock Adam arrived. He stood there in the open door, impeccably dressed as before and looking very pleased to see her. "Come in and see my room," she said. "It's very small but look at the view!" She led him to the window. "It's like living in a stately home here," she said. "Look at the beautiful lawn and gardens where you can wander any time you want. When it's warm some people like to work outside, but I can't concentrate. Does King's have a nice garden?"

"Very nice," said Adam, "I'll show you everything sometime. But now we have to go. We have a reservation at 7:30."

They walked out into the quiet streets. Although it was Saturday night there were few cars on the roads, just some students on bicycles with their obligatory gowns flying behind them. Lucy was still in a state of anxiety, but Adam seemed quite calm. He said, "How do you like Cambridge after Vienna?"

"Oh, I love it here," said Lucy. "I've met lots of people, and there's so much to do. But I must say that in Vienna I felt free for the first time in my life. I felt there was no judgment and I could do just exactly what I wanted. I felt so alive."

"How funny," said Adam, "that's exactly how I felt when I first came to Cambridge. It must be just that when you change countries you don't really belong yet in the new country, so you don't feel bound by the new rules."

"But what about walking on the grass when it says 'Keep off,' and not going down a lane that says 'private way'; don't you feel bound by those sorts of rules?" asked Lucy. "Don't you see that England is so full of rules that you can hardly move without violating one? At home in London I sometimes felt I was living in a cage—though I must admit now that I'm on my own things are easier."

Adam said, "You know, I did walk on the grass in King's where it said 'Keep off,' and a man ran out and told me not to, so now I don't! I agree there are a lot of rules, but they are not really my rules since I'm not English, and so they don't bother me."

By now they had reached the restaurant—a long, low, whitewashed building with Virginia creeper covering the walls. They entered from a little lane and found themselves in a comfortable interior with a low ceiling; a wood fire was blazing, and tables covered with white cloths were set up around it. Each table was lit by a short red candle. The host took their coats and showed them to a table looking out over the river.

Adam drew out Lucy's chair. When she was seated he sat himself opposite her, looking at her with an approving smile.

"Now choose what you want," he said picking up the menu. "Would you like some wine?"

"Oh yes," said Lucy, "and I'll have the steak. I'm always starving for something solid after the mushy food we get at Oldwick." Adam chose a lamb chop for himself and ordered a bottle of red burgundy. Lucy looked at him across the table and smiled. She was in a blur of happiness that she did not know how to contain. At last she felt like a femme fatale, so sophisticated and worldly wise. She sat straight and drank her wine, which made her feel as if she could conquer the world with her charms. "So what rules have you broken in Vienna?" she asked.

"I had an affair with a married woman," he replied.

Lucy was stunned. "What happened?" she asked, dreading the reply.

"She decided to stay with her husband." He looked down at his chop and started to cut it up into little pieces. "Her husband was also my friend before I loved his wife. But now I think less so." Adam said this completely without irony. He looked so serious that Lucy was at a loss for words. She realized that she was out of her depth in a world in which mature people had affairs. She was already jealous of the married woman. Her femme fatale fantasy collapsed. She was just a little girl compared with the sophisticated and certainly beautiful married woman.

"What's her name?" she asked finally in a small voice.

"Gabriele."

In Lucy's beautiful meadow, clouds covered the sun. It seemed to her that the red candle flickered and sank. Her steak seemed less appetizing, and she felt strands of hair begin to escape from her chignon. She would not ask if he still loved Gabriele; it was clear that he did.

The silence between them lengthened. Finally Adam looked across at her and said with a beautiful smile: "But that is in the past; now I am happy to be here with you in beautiful Cambridge." He reached across the table, took her hand, and held it. "This is a wonderful evening," he said. "Drink your wine and we will order some dessert."

Lucy's feelings were in turmoil. There was so much to take in; she no longer knew who she was. She was shocked by the real fact of Adam's past, but at the same time it made him more alluring and drew her into his sophisticated world. Adam squeezed her hand and her spirits soared again. They ate cheesecake for dessert, which reminded Lucy of Vienna. Then Adam said, "Now we will have some coffee and brandy." They moved into another room and sat in two armchairs by the fire. Lucy had never tasted brandy before and sipped it gingerly. It was both fierce and mellow. She loved it; it washed away the sting of Adam's revelation. They started to talk about economics, what Adam was writing in his thesis, and whether they liked their supervisors.

"Miss Mead is very enthusiastic about economic history and the Industrial Revolution," said Lucy. "You can see her glow at the thought that in 1785 after the roads were macadamed, a wagon could travel from London to Newcastle in only three days. This fact has been on my mind since the lecture on Thursday!"

Adam laughed. "My tutorial was all about taxation, but we don't want to talk about that. Let's go for a walk. We still have time." He paid the bill and held her coat for her. Then he took her hand again and they walked out into the crisp, moonlit night. They walked into the center of Cambridge and stood in the marketplace looking at the large bulk of Great St. Mary's Church.

"Are you religious?" asked Lucy.

"I'm a Catholic." Lucy immediately imagined him eating the consecrated bread in St. Stephen's Cathedral in Vienna while a Haydn Mass was played from the gallery. While in Vienna, Lucy had taken to going to mass in St. Stephen's Cathedral whenever music was played. As an Anglican, she did not eat the bread, but there were times when she wanted to.

"But what do you believe about Jesus? Do you believe he is the son of God?"

"Yes," he replied, "I suppose I do. Certainly I have faith in God."

"I think I do too—have faith, I mean," she said, "although God never speaks to me."

"Then maybe you are not listening in the right way," he said.

This seemed like a profound statement to Lucy, although she had not the faintest idea what the right way could be. She said, "Sometimes I try to pray, especially when I'm in church, but I really don't feel as if there's anybody there, so I get discouraged and stop."

Adam looked at her face in the dark. "But everyone gets discouraged," he said. "No one has a straight line to God; we are all struggling."

"Do you think so?" asked Lucy. "It seemed to me that I was always meeting people who were very sure about God. Certainly the people at church when I was a child, and the ladies kneeling and crossing themselves and lighting candles in the Cathedral in Vienna—they didn't seem to struggle at all. But then there was my father, who was very skeptical about God. When I was a child I once asked him if God made the world, and he got very cross and said he could just as well prove to me that Mr. Robinson made the world. I was very confused since I didn't know who Mr. Robinson was. I think he didn't like the church because it is so conservative and bound up with the Tories. He's a socialist, you know; but he never said he was an atheist, just agnostic."

Adam listened to all this thoughtfully and then said, "There is a wonderful book about the spiritual struggle that my mother gave to me when I was seventeen and full of such questions. It is called *Interior Castle* and is written by a sixteenth-century nun called St. Teresa of Avila. She sees a person's struggle to come close to God as a decision to enter her own soul. The soul is full of different rooms (mansions, she calls them), and she must learn to enter and live in each room as she gets closer to the central room, where she can be with God all the time. Now everyone has a soul, but not all decide to enter onto this spiritual path. Maybe you are telling me that that path is for you, Lucy?"

Lucy was silent. She had not expected such a question from this handsome, teasing man who liked to break the rules. She was only just beginning to discover what kind of person he really was, and her fantasy of him was becoming blurred. They were now walking down Botolph's Lane next to St. Bene't's Church. On their right was a low wall, and over the wall they could see the old church cemetery where gravestones with their moss-covered inscriptions stood, lit up in the moonlight. Death seemed to Lucy very far away; she could not imagine it. Adam stopped walking, and they both gazed over the wall. He put his arm round Lucy and began to kiss her lips, first tenderly and then more passionately. "You are lovely," he murmured. Then he put the other arm round her and held her tightly. Lucy felt a rush of love welling up inside her like a great stream flowing from her innermost depths and pouring itself into their embrace. She felt their souls meet and meld as if they could never ever be parted again. They stood locked together for a long time, holding each other close and stroking each other's hair. At last they drew apart, looked at each other, and smiled. They did not speak, though Lucy thought the pounding of her heart could be heard all over Cambridge. They started to walk back toward Oldwick, halting only on the bridge across the Cam. Mist was rising in swirls from the water. As they looked down at the river, two swans swam silently out of the mist toward them. Their stately breasts cut the still water, leaving a gleaming trail of ripples behind them. They swam under the bridge, and Lucy and Adam turned and crossed over to see them swim away.

They reached Oldwick just before the 11:30 curfew. Adam said, "We will see each other again soon, yes?"

"Oh, yes."

3

Fiona

Lucy had heard that the Beatles were coming to Cambridge to give a concert. She was a secret fan. She had been brought up to appreciate strictly classical music, and pop music was regarded at home as childish—not really music at all. But Lucy had heard the Beatles on the radio and had bought a record and thought the songs were wonderful: sweet, innocent, and moving. She very much wanted to go to the concert, but whom could she ask to go with her? She knew Sarah would scoff and ask sarcastically how she could be interested in four little boys; she did not know Anne's tastes at all. But Hannah had seemed calm and friendly and at least she would not be rude, so she walked over to her room in Darwin Hall. She could hear beautiful flute playing inside. Hannah was standing by the window with her flute in front of a tall music stand; she turned as Lucy came in.

"I hope you remember me, I'm Lucy. I do hope I'm not disturbing your practice; you do play well," said Lucy, all in a rush.

"No, no," said Hannah, "Of course I know who you are, and you're not disturbing me at all; I wasn't concentrating anyway."

Hannah was wearing that same patchwork jacket that she had worn at Sarah's Circle, and her hair was scrunched back as it had been then. The parting in the middle was not straight. Lucy disapproved of the hair; she felt Hannah could do something better with it.

"What are you practicing?" she asked, looking at what appeared to be some very difficult music.

"Oh, it's the Shostakovich for the orchestra," said Hannah. "We have a very dour conductor who likes to call randomly on members of the orchestra to play their part by themselves, and I couldn't bear to do it badly in front of the whole crowd."

"That sounds daunting," said Lucy, as Hannah put her flute away and they sat down together. "I say," she went on, "I've just heard that the Beatles are coming to Cambridge. Do you like them? Would you like to go?"

"Are they the group that is causing riots all over the country?" asked Hannah. "I'm not really into pop music, but I must say I did like the songs I heard on the radio. Do you honestly think we can get tickets?"

"Oh, I suppose it will be impossible, but we could just go and see them arrive; don't you think it would be such fun to experience the frenzy?"

"Oh Lucy," replied Hannah laughing, "I don't really think we should get into that mess. At the last concert the police turned hoses on the mob."

"I suppose you're right," said Lucy, "it was just a thought. I'll just try to buy their new record. I do love that song that George sings: 'There were birds in the trees but I never heard them singing, no I never heard them at all till there was you.' Don't you think that's a sweet, simple, true song?" She was thinking, how I wish I could sing this song to Adam to show him how he has changed me.

They talked on about music. Hannah revealed that she loved chamber music and asked Lucy to join a quartet with her and her boyfriend Max, who played the viola. They would play Mozart's flute quartets. Lucy had been hoping that she could find some chamber music at Cambridge and was very flattered to be asked. But they would need a violinist to complete the quartet. After thinking a bit, Hannah said, "Let's ask Fiona Banks. She plays the violin, and she's just down the hall."

Lucy blushed and became a little flustered when she heard this name. She turned away to look out of the window, and there was an awkward pause. Did she really want to see more of Fiona? She thought about the kiss, and then about how familiar Fiona had seemed to be with Adam at that first tea. She couldn't bear it if Adam was interested in anybody but her. Finally, she roused herself from her reverie.

"Oh yes," she said, trying to hide her initial reaction. "I've met Fiona, but I didn't know she played the violin."

"Yes, she does. I haven't actually played with her, but she said something to me at the beginning of term about chamber music, and I never followed up. Why don't we go over to her room now and ask her?"

Fiona was sitting by the fire drinking sherry with Adam. "Hello Hannah, this is a surprise; and you've brought Lucy too—how wonderful!" she gushed. "Now do come and sit down and have a glass of sherry."

Adam had stood up when Hannah and Lucy entered, and now he gave his hand to Hannah and a very big smile to Lucy. Lucy blushed bright red when Adam was introduced; she just couldn't control it, but it mortified her. Fiona gave them each a glass of sherry and said, "We were just talking about Vienna. I know you've been there too, Lucy—isn't it a fantastic city?" Lucy was tongue-tied. Hannah looked at her curiously and, stepping in to fill the gap, asked Fiona whether she would like to join the quartet to play Mozart.

"Oh, I'd love to," said Fiona. "I know the Mozart quartets; they're wonderful and not too dreadfully difficult."

"Do you have an instrument?" asked Hannah, looking at Adam and smiling. "I always think that each person has their own particular instrument hiding inside them and at some time in their childhood this instrument will be revealed. Lucy, you look like a cellist, and Fiona looks like a violinist rather than a cellist, and Max is definitely a viola—but I can't place you, Adam."

"No, no," he said, "I'm just a listener. But I love Mozart, so you will have to perform for me."

"Well, we'll see," Hannah said sweetly in the face of this presumptuous remark. "I don't know if we'll be good enough for you."

"Of course we will," said Fiona, completely missing the irony. "We'll have a performing party and invite all our friends."

During this exchange, Lucy was in agony. She could not bear to sit in the same room as Adam without being able to hold him and kiss him. And what was he doing with Fiona? She looked at her sitting there with a self-satisfied look on her face. Surely he couldn't have kissed Lucy like that if he was with Fiona. Were they just friends? They didn't look like lovers. Lucy finally found her voice and said that she would get the parts from the music shop in Trinity Street so that they could all start practicing. Lucy followed Hannah back to her room and threw herself into a chair.

"I'll just light the fire," said Hannah, "so that we'll be warm until dinner." Then she added, "You seemed a bit taken aback in there. Are you not keen on Fiona?"

"Oh no, Fiona's fine," said Lucy. "I was just a bit surprised to see Adam again; I had met him before at a tea party of Fiona's, and we had a nice conversation."

"What did you think of our discussion at Sarah's about self-doubt?" Hannah asked.

"I don't know," said Lucy. "I have so much myself, I can't imagine what it's like to feel completely confident. How do you do it?"

"Oh, do you think I am confident?" asked Hannah. "Well, that's good, because most of the time I really don't know what I am doing. I just kind of plunge ahead and trust to God to keep me on the straight and narrow. And then, of course I have Max, and he tells me if I am not doing the right thing."

"Do you talk to Max about God?" asked Lucy.

"All the time," said Hannah. "We have great arguments. Usually he wins. But then he's a very serious and brilliant student of theology, and I am not."

"What kind of arguments?" asked Lucy, intrigued by this window into Hannah and Max's relationship.

"The last one was about that strange passage in Luke that says, 'If any man come to me and hate not his father and mother and wife and children and brethren and sisters, yea and his own life also, he cannot be my disciple.' But then there's also that admonition in Matthew that says 'Honor thy father and mother.' So how can these be reconciled? I said that Jesus didn't mean that you had to give up your family, just that you had to separate from them and find your own spiritual place to live. I don't agree with my mother on very much, and I would say we have a pretty thorny relationship, so I can quite see that separating from her is a good thing—but I can still honor her."

"So what does Max argue?"asked Lucy.

"Max says we should be willing to do what Jesus says and literally give up everything to follow him, which is kind of extreme since he has a lovely family. So I said that maybe Jesus was having a bad day and his family was cramping his style when he said that. But Max said I was being flippant and insufficiently reverential."

"So what happened then?" asked Lucy, who was simply dying to know.

"Oh, I don't know," said Hannah. "Max was grumpy for a bit and then it all just blew over."

"Well, religion was not popular in our house, but I always liked it," said Lucy. "Someone told me I should read St. Teresa's *Interior Castle*. I've just started it. Have you read it?"

"No, I haven't," said Hannah, "but I've heard about it. I know it's supposed to be a great mystical treatise."

"Do you think we could discuss it in Sarah's Circle?" asked Lucy.

"You know, the last time I mentioned God, Sarah got very cross," said Hannah, "so how can we possibly persuade her to do this book?"

"Because it was written by a woman for women; I know all the women were nuns, but that doesn't make it any the less a feminist book. Surely the experience of all women is relevant?"

"I see—and after all, why should Sarah always choose the topics?" said Hannah.

"Maybe if you suggested it," ventured Lucy.

As it turned out, Hannah and Lucy saw Sarah at lunch the next day in Hall. Lucy gave Hannah a nudge, and she promptly raised the subject of *Interior Castle*. Sarah was cross, as predicted.

"This is a women's group," she said, "not a séance."

But Hannah was persuasive and emphasized how much Lucy wanted to do the book which was, after all, about women—even if they were nuns. Sarah finally agreed on condition that they also discuss Simone de Beauvoir's book, *The Second Sex*.

Hannah and Lucy looked at each other in triumph and went off to fetch their dessert.

L

4

Disconnection

Lucy was certain now that she was in love with Adam and that she wanted to marry him. She went over and over in her mind the visit with Hannah to Fiona. This was not the way she had wanted to see Adam again, an occasion on which there could be no kiss of welcome, no coming together again, no exchange of confidences. Adam had seemed surprised and pleased to see Lucy enter Fiona's room with Hannah. He had smiled at Lucy in a conspiratorial way, but he received no smile in return. Instead, Lucy had blushed and looked away and not said a word.

Lucy was ashamed of her confusion. She had been so shocked at seeing him again that she had not known how to behave. His smile had somehow made things worse, as if she were to be included in his world with Fiona. Why hadn't he swept her into his arms in front of everyone and claimed her? Instead she had felt exposed and ashamed of what they had experienced together. She found great difficulty in concentrating on her work and even had to sit up very late one night trying to put together an essay for the next day's tutorial because she had been so dilatory. Somehow "Resale Price Maintenance" did not engage her at all.

She did not have long to suffer, for the very next day Adam appeared at her door at tea time wearing an English sports jacket and tie and looking very cheerful.

"I've brought you a copy of the book I was telling you about," he said, and deposited *Interior Castle* in her lap.

"I know I'll love it," she said. She refrained from telling him that she had already started reading a library copy.

Adam sat down in an armchair in front of the fire. He looked around the room, his gaze resting briefly on the pictures of Vienna, pulled on an eyelash to adjust his contact lens, and finally looked back at Lucy.

"Are you staying for tea?" asked Lucy.

"Of course," he said. "That's why I came."

They were both so cool with each other, Lucy could hardly bear it. Why didn't he kiss her? She didn't feel it would be right for her to kiss him, though that was exactly what she wanted to do—to put her arms around him in a passionate embrace. Should she be as cool as he seemed? Or maybe she should try gushing like Fiona? Finally she took refuge in formality.

"It was unexpected seeing you yesterday at Fiona's.

"Yes it was," he said, "but very nice for me to see you there. Fiona and I have been friends for quite a while. She has spent some time in Vienna too, and I met her there. But you are a new friend."

"Oh," said Lucy; she did not feel reassured.

"I shall be interested to see how the quartet works out," he said, crossing a leg and smoothing his trousers.

"I think it will be fun," said Lucy.

"A violinist I once knew claimed that playing chamber music was better than making love, but I can't believe that," he said, looking at Lucy with a smile. Lucy hid her shock and looked back at him with a steady gaze. She could not claim to know about actually making love, but she did love the extraordinary musical connection that chamber music fostered among the players. So she said, "Maybe it comes in second."

Adam laughed and held out his cup for more tea. "Well, I wish I could do it," he said. "The chamber music, I mean."

Lucy still felt disconnected. She took a different tack. "Could we talk about economics sometime? I'm having difficulty with the theory we're doing now. I can't work out the role of real wages in the Keynesian model. Somehow Miss Mead is not very clear."

Adam laughed, "Oh, you mean as opposed to money wages, not unreal wages!"

Lucy thought this was rather witty. She looked at Adam in the hopes of finding something romantic in his amusement but was disappointed.

"Well, any time you like," said Adam, but he made no further comment on her problem and did not look eager to pursue the topic. Perhaps he does not know the answer thought Lucy suddenly, and was then shocked at her own thought. Surely Adam must know everything.

The sun was setting, and it was getting dark. As Lucy gazed out of the window she saw the gardens disappearing into the mist. Adam was silent and so was she. Lucy felt a tension rise between them as if they were at cross purposes; she had no idea what Adam was expecting from her. Eventually he got up, walked over to her, and put his hand on her shoulder. "I've got work to do in the library before dinner. Thanks for the tea." He bent down and kissed her cheek and left.

Lucy looked at the closing door as if it were shutting out all her dreams. She looked down and found she was still holding *Interior Castle*. She opened Adam's gift, found her place, and returned to St. Teresa.

At dinner that night she found herself sitting between Sarah and Anne. Anne was wearing the same dress she had worn at Sarah's Circle; it was looking a little grubby. The hall was brightly lit, and the long tables were filled with girls all chattering away like a flock of birds. Lucy was eating her steamed pudding and custard with relish. It was her favorite pudding. Her father's, too. She turned to Anne and said, "I never asked you what you were reading, do tell me."

"I'm reading English, like Sarah," replied Anne in her timid voice.

"Yes," said Sarah breaking in, "and we were just talking about the nineteenth century."

"Have you read *Shirley* too?" asked Lucy, turning toward Anne again.

"Yes," said Anne, "and I find it is a very strange book. There are two heroines and both are in love, but both find marriage a very unsatisfactory idea because of the power the husband has over his wife. It seems that being in love leads them both to a very difficult choice."

"I suppose it might," said Lucy blushing. She was in love and was quite sure that she would do anything for Adam. She didn't feel that independence from him was a desirable state. Quite the contrary, she wanted her life to be totally bound up with his. Of course, he had power over her, but she did not disdain it, as she knew Sarah and Anne would. She could not articulate for herself the idea that love is a risky business, but she knew she was ready for anything with Adam.

"It's the idea of being in love that's the problem," said Sarah. "It's such a demeaning frame of mind. You idealize and worship the man you love so you can't see your real self at all. At least that's what I've observed of people who claim to be in love. They just literally lose their reason. I've never been in love and don't intend to be," she concluded firmly.

"I suppose Sarah is right," said Anne, reaching for the custard jug, "though it must be nice to have a partner. But in my parents' marriage it is always my mother who lays down the law and my father who goes along with it. He is a 'peace at any price' person. But isn't there room for equality between two people?"

"Not in a patriarchal society," said Sarah. "Every institution is set up to favor men. Look at how many men there are at Cambridge compared with women. There are just three women's colleges and more than twenty for men, and I can't believe that it's because men are so much cleverer than women."

Lucy was depressed by this conversation. Evidently Sarah viewed being in love as some kind of sickness, whereas to her it was the opening of a new world of feeling and connection. Then she thought of Adam's coolness to her this afternoon and felt even lower. Lucy thought marriage to Adam would be like heaven. She put it in a category completely separate from that of her parents or other older people that she knew. Her total inexperience of relationships with men meant that she had only her fantasies to go on. For her a relationship meant simply being with Adam and doing things with him. She did not think about the time when their opinions had clashed. So at this moment she found Sarah's dogmatic, anti-male views extremely distasteful. Ironically, Lucy saw Sarah's view of men as oppressors as quite unrealistic, almost fantastical. Also, she thought Sarah was patronizing to Anne, an exercise of power that contradicted everything Sarah had been saying. Lucy finished her pudding, got up to go before the grace was said, bowed to the Principal on high table, and took herself back to her room where she could settle down by the fire and be alone with her thoughts.

She imagined what a life with Adam would be like. Of course, she would live wherever he wanted (she hoped that would be Vienna) and support him in whatever job he chose. They would travel and see the world. She had no idea what she would do in the way of work. In fact, the idea of working, apart from her studies, seemed alien to her. No one ever talked about having a career except those girls who were going to become doctors or teachers. Most of the girls seemed to get married right after Cambridge, and that was Lucy's goal. Once married, she would simply keep the house and tend to the children. She would at last have found a man whom she could love wholeheartedly and who would love her. They would have a home together. She would furnish her house in Austria in the Beidermeier style: cozy furniture, flowers, and pictures on the walls of bucolic scenes.

After a while, she roused herself and began to think about where things actually stood with Adam; they did not seem to be moving toward marriage. He had indeed brought her the book, but he had also been so cool. He had kissed her cheek but not her lips. She did not understand how it could be he had not wanted to renew their passion. He had seemed interested in her spiritual life and thought that this must surely be a sign of love. She clung to that. Once again, she took up her book and continued to read.

5

The Beatles

The next day Lucy woke up feeling low. It was only nine o'clock, and her next lecture was not until 10:30, but rather than spend time in the library she decided to pamper herself and cycled off to the Copper Kettle for a cup of coffee. As she sipped her coffee, she glanced at the local paper someone had left on her table. The headlines were full of the Beatles due to appear at the Regal, a large cinema outside the center of Cambridge. How she would love to hear them, she thought. She had never been to a pop concert and had no idea what it would be like. She had given way to Hannah's doubts about the crowds, but now she thought she might try to go on her own to cheer herself up and to take her mind off Adam. She saw that the box office for tickets for tomorrow's concert opened at ten; of course she would have to go early. Feeling very pleased to have made this decision, she reached her lecture on time and spent the rest of the day in pleasant anticipation.

In the morning she arose at 6:00 and cycled some distance to the Regal. Her heart sank as she saw a crowd of people already there. The queue for tickets snaked around the building. "Oh well," she thought, "I expected this." She locked her bike and joined the vast queue ready for the long wait. She hoped that the tickets would not all be sold when her turn came. Next to her stood a woman with two young daughters who couldn't have been more than fourteen. The woman smiled at Lucy and asked, "Are you here by yourself?"

"Oh yes, of course," Lucy replied, "I'm a student here, at Oldwick College."

"My goodness," said the woman, "You don't look old enough for that."

Behind Lucy the queue was rapidly growing. She turned around to see how long it was now and saw a group of undergraduates laughing and talking together. They were passing a thermos round and seemed much more prepared for the long wait than Lucy. Lucy looked at the thermos longingly. Just then the woman in front said, "Would you like some of our tea? I've brought a big thermos, and there's enough for four. Lucy gratefully accepted, and the wait seemed much more tolerable. At long last she became the triumphant owner of a single ticket to the Beatles, which she guarded with her life.

When she returned that night the crowd was back jostling around the entrance to the theatre and spilling out into the street. It consisted largely of very young girls who shrieked a lot and pushed each other around. Adults seemed to be absent except for the undergraduates scattered among them. Lucy pushed her way toward the entrance, ticket in hand. Just as she was about to reach the door a girl behind her grabbed her ticket and vanished inside with it. "Hey, hey,"cried Lucy, "that's my ticket—give it back!" She realized she was shouting but could not stop herself. She tried to follow the girl but was prevented by the crowd. Suddenly a man standing at the door pushed his way toward her and said, "I saw that, duckie. These people are like animals. Come with me, love, I'll help you get in."

Lucy stopped shouting and looked at him. He was short and compact in his suit and tie, and looked like a gnome. He had long, bushy black hair that fell to his shoulders, and his eyes were dark and bright. His enormous eyebrows were joined together at the top of a long nose. Above a cleft chin, his lopsided mouth was smiling at Lucy, and she instinctively trusted him. He found her hand and pulled her out of the crowd toward the side of the theatre. "This way," he said. "I'll let you in the side door; I'm the manager here." He opened the door and pushed her in ahead of him. They stood in a dark corridor and could hear the noise of the crowds inside and outside the building. "You look like a nice girl." he said. "How would you like to sit near the front? I'll let you have my seat and I can stand at the back—not that you'll be doing much sitting!"

"Oh," said Lucy who was in a state of great confusion. "That's so kind of you—I thought I would miss the concert when that girl took my ticket. Thank you very much."

"Well, come with me, my love," said the gnome. Lucy realized that he still held her hand in his. She held on tightly and followed him down the corridor. He pulled a curtain aside and they stood in the dimly lit auditorium already full of people. The cinema was huge; it had evidently been built in the 1930s when films were coming into their own. It was painted dark purple. Two majestic green lions supported square columns on either side of the green velvet curtain in front of which a large stage had been constructed. Microphones, loudspeakers, and a set of drums were waiting for the performers. To Lucy, it felt like a temple. The gnome pushed his way to the front and showed Lucy to a seat in the second row. "There you are now," he said. "I'll be keeping an eye on you." He finally let go her hand and called to her as he pushed his way out of the row: "The name's Danny."

Lucy sat down in her seat to catch her breath. She realized she was very lucky. All around her young girls were already dancing. They wore miniskirts and thin cardigans and were jumping up and down, clasping each other in crazy anticipation. Finally the lights dimmed, and Danny appeared on the stage waving his hands to calm the noise. In spite of his strange looks he radiated energy and good cheer. "I am proud," he said, "very proud that our theatre can bring to you the most amazing group ever to come to Cambridge. I present to you, THE BEATLES!"

And there they were, each one slimmer than the next, bobbing onto the stage with their guitars, and their neatly cut hair. Waves of noise greeted them. Everyone was up in their rows waving their hands and yelling. Lucy stood up too and clapped.

They started singing. The beat was loud; their voices were warm and insistent. Their songs were all about love and longing. "Love, love me do, you know I'll be true, so please, please love me." Then again: "Love, love, love. All you need is love. Love is all you need." And then more boldly: "And when I touch you I feel happy inside, It's such a feeling that my love I can't hide." Lucy couldn't believe her ears. Here were these sweet swaying boys singing about her, her love for Adam and her longing to be loved in return. But to them love was not shameful, not something to be hidden away and suffered, it was glorious, to be shouted from the rooftops. I love you, so please love me back. It was the insistence that love is demanding, that longing for love is wonderful not shameful, that moved her to tears. She was up now in her seat singing along and waving with all the other girls. Her body was alive and tingling all over; she felt the same feelings she had felt when she had kissed Adam back. Her longing for him was immense, but now it was joyous and thrilling.

The concert went on for what seemed like hours, and Lucy became hoarse from shouting and singing. Finally the show was over and the crowd rushed for the doors to try to see the singers as they left in their car. Lucy walked outside slowly. She was dazed and overwhelmed. She started looking around vaguely for her bike and glanced at her watch. Oh God, she thought, I've got only half an hour until the college closes. She felt a hand touch her arm; it was Danny. "And how did you like the Beatles, little Miss?" he asked. Lucy turned around, looked at his laughing face, and laughed too. "Oh, they were electrifying; I was quite shaken," she said.

"Yes," he said, "and they're going to be even bigger, you mark my words."

"Ah, there it is," said Lucy as she finally spotted her bike. She started undoing the padlock. "How about a drink then?" asked Danny, taking her completely by surprise. She looked at him as if for the first time. His face seemed to glow with goodness. She had no idea how old he was. "Oh, I can't," she said, "I've got to be back at Oldwick College in half an hour or I'll get locked out. But thanks for all you've done." He looked at her as if measuring her up. "All right, duckie, maybe some other time." She felt him watching her as she rode away and waved back at him.

A few days later, she came out of her morning lecture and decided to zip into Heffers bookshop to buy a copy of Dostoyevsky's *Crime and Punishment*. She had heard some girls talking about it at dinner and thought that she should educate herself. She found it on the shelf and began to read the first page. "Redemption," said a voice behind her. "There is forgiveness!" She knew who it was before she looked up, and saw Danny beside her. "Oh Danny," she said, "how funny to see you here, but then such coincidences always happen, don't they? Just when you've met someone you immediately see them again. Thanks so much again for giving me your ticket."

"Well, I couldn't let you miss it now, could I?" he asked.

"So you know *Crime and Punishment*?" she asked. "Do you like the book?"

"One of the greats," he replied. "You'll like his books, though they are sometimes hard to read."

"You sound as if you read a lot," said Lucy. She thought it odd that the theatre manager was a reader. It had never occurred to her that anybody outside her own small, educated acquaintance would read.

"What's your name, duckie?" he asked. "Would you like to have a quick coffee? There's a little place round the corner."

"I'm Lucy," she said, looking at her watch. She had to get back to college for lunch, and then there was a quartet rehearsal in the afternoon. But she felt she could not turn him down again. So she said, "I'd love to, I've just got time." But what were they going to talk about?

Danny slurped his coffee and dunked a large biscuit into it, completely at ease. His eyes looked at Lucy with a friendly, searching gaze. He asked her what she did, and Lucy found herself telling him about her family and what it was like to be at college in her very first term. "It's all very busy and confusing," she said. "I've made some new friends, but of course you can never really know what people are like when you've known them only a short time." She was thinking particularly of Adam.

"You'll have to wait to find out—you'll have to learn to wait," said Danny. "Much of life is waiting, really, isn't it? Waiting for the kettle to boil, waiting for the bus, waiting for the holidays, waiting for love, waiting for happiness, waiting for God. The Beatles' songs are all about waiting for love; I think that's why I like them so much."

Lucy's eyes flew up to his face. "Oh, so do I," she said. "Sometimes I feel as if I am waiting to find myself because I'm not really here yet." Then she stopped. She couldn't believe she was talking about her innermost thoughts to a complete stranger. But then Danny did not feel like a stranger at all.

"Oh you're here all right, love," he said smiling at her. Then he told her about his life. His father had worked in a shoe factory and then set up a small shoe repair shop in Cambridge before he became too ill to continue working. His mother was the daughter of a Methodist minister. When he left school at sixteen he worked with his father for a while repairing shoes. "Did you know that there are forty-four steps involved in making a lace-up shoe?" he asked. He was interested in films and wanted to go into the film business. So far the closest he had come was managing the Regal cinema. But he had some contacts and was hoping to move to London soon, where the films were made. He was an expert on films, he reckoned, since he had seen so many. The difficulty would be finding a job in films that paid enough to live on.

Lucy listened with fascination. She had never talked to anyone like Danny before. She looked at her watch. "I'm terribly sorry, but I've got to go," she said.

"So do I," Danny replied. "I hope you'll have coffee with me again sometime."

"Oh yes, I'd like that," said Lucy. "You can find me at Oldwick, Lucy Page."

"And I'm Danny Martin. You know where to find me."

What an extraordinary person, thought Lucy, as she cycled back to Oldwick for lunch. His strange looks and his direct way had made a deep impression on her. She hoped she would see him again.

6

The Quartet

Of course Fiona was late; Lucy had almost expected it. She herself had arrived on time at two o'clock in the music room in Oldwick. It was just large enough for the players and had a nice grand piano which they did not need but was convenient for tuning. Hannah and her boyfriend Max were already there when Lucy arrived with her cello and ancient folding music stand. She was extremely eager to be there, not only for the music but because she wanted to meet Max.

Max smiled cordially at Lucy and continued to tune his viola. Lucy was intrigued; he had a large frame and was very tall, with a pleasant face and a serious, even pompous, expression. He had bushy brown hair and large brown eyes, and his smile was gentle and slightly mocking. He was dressed in a shabby tweed jacket over an old shirt and tie. He had the same comfortable air as Hannah. He was nothing like Adam, whose handsome face and impeccable dress delighted Lucy. But Hannah was looking at him proudly, and they seemed to be comfortable with each other. They talked about the orchestra as they adjusted their chairs and seemed for a moment to be oblivious of Lucy.

Lucy sat down, looked over the music that she had been practicing, and began tuning her instrument, taking her "A" from Hannah. She always seemed to take much longer than everyone else. When she had finally finished she looked up. Hannah and Max both started practicing the difficult passages, so Lucy joined in, and there was a cacophony as each played different parts. After about ten minutes Hannah stopped and said, "I don't know where Fiona has got to; I'm sure I said Friday at two."

Max said, "If she's always going to be late, we've got a problem."

"Oh no," said Lucy immediately, "I'm sure there's a good explanation. I hope nothing serious has happened to her."

Lucy was at heart a peacemaker, and this led her to defend Fiona. But then she immediately regretted it, thinking "She's not my friend after all."

"Well, let's start without her," said Hannah, "top of the first movement." She raised her flute, looked at Max and Lucy to see that they were ready, counted "one, two, three, four" to give the tempo, and off they went into the first lovely melody. Lucy played her best, using all the musical skills that Professor Pracht had given her, and Hannah and Max were in top form. It all sounded very nice, except for the absence of the violin, which Lucy found increasingly annoying. Where was Fiona? They had just started a run-through of the second movement, a flute solo playing the melody accompanied by pizzicato in the strings, when the door opened and Fiona rushed in, completely out of breath. Hannah and Max kept on playing, but Lucy couldn't help but stop to greet her.

"Am I terribly late?" Fiona gasped, in a voice even more gushy than usual because of the breathlessness. "I was having lunch with friends and just couldn't get away. It would have been much better if we'd decided to start at 2:30. Let's do that next time."

Hannah looked very cross. "We've started without you," she said in a stern tone. "But we're very glad you're here now," said Lucy, with a friendlier voice. Lucy was annoyed that Fiona hadn't apologized for being late, and she remembered that other time when Fiona had also failed to apologize when she spilled tea on Camilla's skirt. But still she smiled at Fiona to defuse the tension. Max, appearing not to feel any of the annoyance of Hannah and Lucy, just nodded to Fiona and shifted his chair to let her in. Then he took up a pipe and began to fill it. While Hannah was handing Fiona the music, Max struck a match, lit his pipe, and started to puff away. He said, "Let's start again from the beginning." Lucy was amazed and wondered how he could possibly play with a pipe in his mouth, while admitting to herself that she found the whole thing very attractive. She quite liked the smell of the smoke; the pipe gave Max an unmistakable air of authority. As it turned out, his playing seemed completely unaffected.

This time the music sounded as Mozart had written it, though Lucy soon discovered that Fiona was not, in fact, a very good player. She had obviously not practiced her part. She was often out of tune, and many of the running passages were muddy; but the worst thing was that she was not an inherently musical player, and had no nuance. At the end of the first passage (which she had not managed well), Fiona interrupted and said, "Let's play that again at half time so that we can all get the notes." So they tried again. Then Fiona said, "And once more"—and they all dutifully followed along, the others playing their part perfectly while Fiona worked out her own. No one did anything to stop Fiona usurping Hannah's role as leader, but after about an hour the piece was starting to sound quite good.

They played the second movement with the melody in the flute and pizzicato for the strings. "Well done, Hannah," said Max when they were finished. Hannah looked back at Max, and love was in her face. Lucy thought, "They are so lucky; they have love and chamber music at the same time." Her curiosity about Hannah and Max was intense. She wondered whether they felt passion between them. They both seemed so steady and unemotional. She wondered whether they kissed and what the pipe tasted like. She found herself envying the fact they looked like an old married couple but at the same time thinking that this kind of passionless familiarity was not what she wanted at all.

Then Hannah got up and declared that she had to go to a tutorial, and so there was no time for the third movement. Turning to Fiona, she said, "Do you think you can make it at 2:00 next week, or shall we say 2:15?" Fiona had the nerve to look put out that her suggestion of 2:30 had not been followed but replied, "I suppose 2:15 would be all right."

As they were leaving, Fiona said to Lucy, "Would you like to come and have tea with me now? You know where I am in Darwin." Lucy was surprised; she did not think she was Fiona's type, not like the silk blouse women she had met at that first tea. However, she could not think of a reason to say no, so she said,

"Yes, I'd like that very much. Shall I come with you now?"

Fiona seemed pleased, and they walked together to her room. Lucy sat on the floor by the fire and Fiona started boiling a kettle, putting tea in a pot and getting out cups and saucers. She went to a cupboard and took out a cake tin from which she produced a delicious-looking marble cake.

"Look what I've got here," she said gaily, cutting Lucy a large slice. She filled the teapot, waited two minutes by the clock, and then poured the tea, which was nice and strong, just as Lucy liked it. Lucy was beginning to feel quite cozy and comfortable, when Fiona said casually, "Have you seen much of Adam?" Lucy tried hard to control a blush.

"No," she replied. Her parents had regarded lying as a terrible thing, but it did not occur to Lucy to tell Fiona the truth. She could not say that she and Adam had kissed passionately and then that Adam had been so cool. She could not admit that they had had a talk about spiritual things and that Adam had given her a book. Most of all she could not reveal her deepest desire, to become Adam's wife.

"Oh," said Fiona, looking relieved. "Well I just wondered. You seemed to have a nice conversation with him when I first introduced you."

"Yes, we did," said Lucy, relieved to be able to say something truthful, "but he seems to be a busy person."

"Oh yes, he is," said Fiona, "but he often comes here for tea, and we have good talks. Has he given you a book? He gave me the poems of Rilke in German, but I'm afraid my German is not as good as he seems to think, though I have read one or two with the help of a dictionary."

Lucy was silent about her book even though she was mortified that Fiona had received one too. She was not in charge of her feelings; they were all in a muddle. She was, in fact, dismissing the thought that Adam and Fiona could be anything more than just good friends and was deeply upset that Adam seemed to regard his friendship with her in the same light. These feelings made her feel very uncomfortable.

Thankfully, since Lucy remained silent, Fiona changed the subject. "You know Sarah Hardy, don't you? I know Hannah is in her Circle because she's told me about it. Have you been to any of the meetings? Do you enjoy them?"

"I've been to only one so far," said Lucy, "and I've talked a lot with Sarah and the other girls at lunch and dinner. We discussed self-doubt, and everyone had a lot to say."

"How fascinating," said Fiona. "In Darwin we talk mainly about our work, our tutors, and other people. I don't know what I would say about self-doubt. What did you say?"

Lucy gave Fiona what she thought was an accurate description of the various points of view discussed in the circle. She saw Fiona wrinkle up her face in disapproval as she described Sarah's views of the exploitation of women by men. "But I am in favor of marriage," Fiona protested at one point, "and I have lots of relationships with other people. So I must be a secure person according to your view, Lucy." Lucy decided she had said enough about the Circle and did not comment any further. She realized that she had taken a dislike to Fiona because of Adam. After all, Fiona had clearly invited her in order to go on a fishing expedition. Lucy was depressed at the thought that she and Fiona were in the same category with Adam.

"I'll be late for dinner," she said. "Thanks so much for the lovely tea."

"It was nothing," replied Fiona coolly.

7

Max

Lucy spent the next few days going to lectures, working at her desk in Oldwick, and thinking of Adam. She looked back over the last two encounters and found herself at sea. But the memory of the kiss reassured her that this was surely love; what else could it be? Then she thought of Danny's words about waiting. That's what she was doing, waiting for Adam to declare himself.

These thoughts so disturbed her concentration that she got up, put her work away, and started to walk over to the Buttery. On the way she bumped into Hannah, who was looking very cross, with a frown on her face and her mouth turned down, quite unlike the pleasant, equable Hannah she thought she knew.

"What's the matter?" she asked. "You look very down in the dumps."

"Oh dear," replied Hannah, "is it that obvious?"

"Oh no," said Lucy, "only you usually look so cheerful. Has anything happened?"

"Well, in a way, I suppose you could say that it has—but never mind about that."

"Can I help?" asked Lucy.

"No, not really, it's just that Max is so obtuse at times I could strangle him."

As she said this Hannah's frown deepened.

"Look," said Lucy, "I was just walking over to the Buttery to get a cup of coffee. Maybe you'd like to come with me so we can talk."

Hannah hesitated; then she said, "Yes, all right, I'd like that very much."

The Buttery was a new coffee shop in a big modern building next to the Marshall Library, where Lucy often worked. It had rather a bland décor: white walls and cafeteria-style tables. But it served delicious tea, coffee, and cakes and was almost always full. The bustle and chatter made Lucy feel as if she were in the center of things. They found a table and sat down with their coffee. Lucy asked, "What's wrong with Max, Hannah?"

"Well, it's hard to know where to begin. Max and I were having tea together, and we were talking about the quartet—you know, how one does go over events afterward. And it was all very friendly. We agreed that you are a jolly good player, and Max said he thought you had excellent rhythm and a very good sound."

"Well, that's very nice of you," said Lucy. "The sound comes from Professor Pracht in Vienna, with his special bowing technique."

"But we thought Fiona was going to be a better player than she was," said Hannah, "though after we had gone over things slowly it all sounded much better. I hope she practices between rehearsals. Then we began to talk about the orchestra and the difficult pieces we are playing. The Shostakovich Symphony No. 5 is wonderful but really hard for the flute; you know what I mean because you heard me practicing it the other day, and the Strauss oboe concerto is even worse. I sit next to Jeremy, who makes so many mistakes even though he is the first flute, and I am always covering for him. And then it occurred to me that I should be first flute, not Jeremy. So I said this to Max, and at first he didn't even respond to my remark, but just said he thought my playing in the flute quartet was wonderful, which was nice. Then I repeated my comment, and he just said that Jeremy is in his third year and came up through the ranks, and I was only in my second year. So I said that I play so much better than Jeremy, surely the conductor could see that I should be in the first chair. Max seemed rather put out and said he hadn't realized that I was so ambitious, as if ambition was a bad thing. Then I suddenly realized that there wasn't a single woman in the first chair in the whole orchestra."

"Well, I dare say there is not," said Lucy, "but isn't that just because there are very few women in the orchestra?"

"That's the whole point, don't you see? Max even said that he thought that Jeremy was first because the conductor, Jonathan, and he had known each other before and I would have to wait for my turn. But that's what women have been doing for centuries, and they never get anywhere. Max says the orchestra is a hierarchy, not a democracy, but I think it's the working of the patriarchy, just as Sarah says. It's power before art. And I got so frustrated because Max didn't even acknowledge the point I was making." Tears came to Hannah's eyes.

At first Lucy didn't know at all what to say. The whole thing was so mixed up. She knew that she was on Hannah's side where the argument was concerned but thought that Hannah had been very provocative. Hannah clearly felt very strongly about being first flute, strongly enough to cry about it. But this seemed a bit like a regurgitation of Sarah's preaching, and Lucy had still not been convinced by Sarah's arguments. So she said, "Well, I do see how difficult it all is. How did you leave things with Max?"

"He just changed the subject and said I was making good progress on his jumper, wasn't I? I was ready to drop all my stitches on purpose, but then he left. Sarah thinks women could do without men entirely, and I'm beginning to think she's right."

"But that's ridiculous," said Lucy, glad of the chance to rebut Sarah's extreme thinking. "I like men and don't see how one can rule out half the human race, apart from the fact that no babies would be born. Sarah's wrong on that."

Hannah was silent; her tears overflowed, and she brushed at them like annoying flies. Lucy saw that she had been wrong in pushing Hannah's anger and frustration away so fast. She tried to redeem the situation. "What I mean is that of course you should be first chair; you play so beautifully, and Max should see that." She stumbled on, "I wish I could be of more help, but I'm afraid I don't know much about men at all. I really like Adam, but I just don't know whether he likes me in the same way or not." She trailed off; she certainly wasn't going to reveal the kiss to Hannah.

"Oh, I'm sure he does," said Hannah, in an offhand way. Lucy saw that Hannah was still thinking about Max. This was clearly not the time to talk to her about Adam. A gloomy silence settled between them as each considered her own predicament. Lucy was intrigued by Hannah's relationship with Max. Hannah had seemed unexpectedly passionate in her feelings about her position in the orchestra; Lucy had thought she was more even-tempered. But then Max had not been sympathetic, and Lucy wondered why. Being in a relationship with a man seemed to be like navigating dangerous shoals; one never knew when one would capsize.

Finally, Lucy said, "Well, I've had an idea that I was thinking about when I bumped into you. Let's have a dinner party with the Circle and we'll invite Adam and Max (even though they are being difficult). That makes seven of us with Sarah, Anne, and Charlotte, though if we ask them each to bring a guest it will be a bit of a squash. We can set up two tables together in my room and cook something exotic in the kitchen. Don't you think it would be fantastic?"

Hannah looked up from her coffee and a different expression came across her face. "You are brave," she said. "I'd no idea you would think up something like that. I'd love to do it."

"I'll send out the invitations," said Lucy, "and you start looking for recipes."

Lucy was extremely pleased with herself. The idea of the dinner party had come to her that morning. Her parents often had dinner parties, and Lucy had always thought they were festive and sophisticated. Now Adam could be seen as her friend and her friend alone. They would appear together in public like a couple, as if Adam were part of her everyday life in which they always did things together.

She wrote out the invitations on white cards that she hoped the recipients would display on their mantelpieces with other invitations for their visitors to read, as was the custom. Some girls had mantelpieces that were filled with cards, and others had only a few. Lucy was in the latter group, but now she was actually giving a party so she did not mind. Now she too would be on the social map. On the invitations for Sarah, Charlotte, and Anne, she wrote "and guest." She decided to work out the table arrangement later.

Sarah interrupted her task. Lucy hadn't really talked to Sarah since she had suggested *Interior Castle* for the Circle, and she was pleased to see her. "I hope I'm not disturbing you," said Sarah.

"No, not at all," said Lucy. "I was just writing out some invitations. Here's yours." She handed the white card to Sarah, who looked at it with interest.

"How lovely," said Sarah sitting on a chair for a change, "a dinner party! Well I can certainly come on that day, but I won't bring a guest; I'd much rather just come by myself. How on earth are you going to manage the cooking?"

"The kitchen's just across the hall, and Hannah is going to find a recipe. I think she's probably a very good cook," said Lucy.

"Have you invited the whole Circle?" asked Sarah.

"Oh yes, of course," said Lucy, "and one or two other people as well."

For a moment Sarah looked intrigued; then she changed the subject. "I just came over to let you know that I've read *Interior Castle,*" she said. "I really don't know what to say about it, or whether we should discuss it in the Circle at all. I'm not religious, so I found it very hard going. And I got so impatient with the references to God as 'His Majesty.'"

"But there are so many interesting things in the book about the search for the self and soul," said Lucy. "Don't you think that's what the task is for people, to find themselves?"

"I think St. Teresa loses rather than finds herself," said Sarah. "It's as if she's in love with God. So I thought, if we are to discuss the book at all, we should do it at the same time as we discuss de Beauvoir."

"All right," said Lucy, "let's do both books together and see what the others have to say."

"Fine," said Sarah. She got up, hiked up her skirt that was trailing on the ground, and left.

Lucy completed her invitations and went down to the Porter's lodge to post them.

8

The Dinner Party

"Look, Woolworth's!" cried Hannah, triumphantly holding up two aprons made of thin cotton with very large, bright flowers all over them. "Now we can begin." She and Lucy were getting ready for the big dinner party. Their excitement that Adam and Max were coming knew no bounds. Now they could show how clever they were, how well organized, how sophisticated. Lucy finally had a way of giving her love for Adam a concrete expression. She was concerned that Adam would not like the dinner because he was so used to the lovely Austrian cuisine. But she was longing for the chance to cook for him, to offer him something delicious that she had made so that he could picture her as his wife. They decided to stick to basics as all the recipes Hannah produced seemed too complicated: sole in a white cheese sauce that Lucy had learned how to make from her mother; roast potatoes, more elegant than mashed; and green beans cut on the cross in the French style. Hannah had suggested peas, but Lucy said hastily, "Oh I can't stand the kind that are not properly cooked and rattle onto the plate, or they're the mushy green blobs we get at dinner." So beans it was. For dessert, they decided to splurge on a gateau from the smart pastry shop "Fitzbillies" opposite the Fitzwilliam museum.

"I'll ask Max to choose the wine," said Hannah.

"That's fine," said Lucy and went off to do the shopping while Hannah was dispatched to find two baking pans. When they returned they set up three card tables and some chairs from the all-purpose room and covered the tables with a white sheet of Lucy's. There would be eight people round the table: Sarah and the whole Circle, Adam and Max, and an unidentified guest whom Anne had surprisingly said she would bring. Charlotte was coming alone like Sarah. "I just don't *know* any nice men well enough to ask," she had told Lucy, "I *wish* I did." They could all just fit round the table and still have room for the door to open.

They prepared the meal well in advance and, having put everything in the oven to keep warm, they rushed back to their rooms to change for dinner. Lucy's red sheath dress was brought out again, and she put her hair up in a chignon, just as she had done when she had dinner with Adam on the blissful night of the kiss. She powdered her face and put on some lipstick—she had only just started wearing makeup. The girl looking back at her in the mirror was pretty she thought, and then pushed the thought away. She had never been complimented on her looks and thought there must be something vain about wanting to look nice. Nevertheless, she smiled at herself as she pushed a lock out of her eyes. Hannah returned wearing a large green raw silk blouse over her long skirt; she had her hair down, the first time Lucy had seen it that way. It was fine and silky. "You look wonderful," said Lucy approvingly.

Sarah arrived promptly at 7:30 with Max right behind her, carrying some wine bottles. "We met at the top of the stairs and guessed we were going to the same room," said Max. He said a warm hello to Lucy and then gazed at Hannah. "I've never seen your hair like that before," he said, "it's lovely," and kissed her cheek. Hannah blushed and looked pleased. Lucy thought that Hannah seemed to have forgiven him for the spat about Jeremy. She took the wine from Max and handed him a glass of sherry. She gave one to Sarah too, and then she poured herself a glass and took a big sip. The warmth slid down her throat. She relished her role as hostess in charge of the guests; it made her feel powerful. She was willing to put herself forward and take charge.

Just then Anne arrived looking flushed and happy as she produced her guest, Jeremy. Hannah nearly choked on her sherry. Anne was dressed this time in a pleated skirt and jumper. Lucy thought it strange that she wore dresses for everyday and a skirt and jumper for best. She welcomed Jeremy, who looked about fourteen, had a pimpled face and greasy fair hair. He was sporting a bow tie and looked very pleased to have been included in the party. "Well, this is jolly nice," he said as he shook Lucy's hand, looking at her in a frank and open way. "Hello Hannah, hello Max, long time no see. And this must be Sarah. I recognize you from Anne's description; she talks about you all the time." Sarah looked as if she didn't know whether to be pleased or annoyed by this address; she nodded at Jeremy, took out a cigarette, lit it, and blew the smoke toward him. She said to Anne, "I'd no idea you knew anybody."

Lucy was busy pouring sherry for Jeremy and fruit juice for Anne when she felt an arm being put around her waist from behind. Another arm thrust a bouquet of flowers in front of her. For a minute all she could see were the flowers bobbing away. Then, with her heart in her mouth she turned, and there was Adam, smiling at her.

"These flowers reminded me of you," he said. Before she could speak, Charlotte's booming voice said, "I suppose I'm the last one—I'm *always* late." Charlotte came and stood right in front of Adam, so Lucy introduced them and was forced to leave them while she got them some sherry and then went to the kitchen to find a vase for the flowers; they were anemones. There was no vase, so Lucy put them in a glass and returning, placed them in the middle of the table where they looked very fine. She wanted to return to Adam's side but saw that he was deep in conversation with Charlotte while Sarah was standing all on her own, smoking. Anne, Jeremy, Hannah, and Max were engaged in conversation together. Hannah still looked put out by the presence of Jeremy, but the others were talking and laughing. Lucy went over to Sarah. "Let's go and join the others," she said and steered a reluctant Sarah over to the group. Jeremy was saying, "I'm so glad I sit next to Hannah in the orchestra, she gets all the rhythms right."

"I'm sure she does," said Max, "and everything else, too."

"Well, the Shostakovich is so difficult you just have to practice it at home," said Hannah looking directly at Jeremy.

"You bet," he said vaguely; turning to Anne, "Now tell me more about this Circle of yours." Lucy could see Sarah's hackles rise; it was her Circle, after all. Anne said innocently, "Well we read books about women and for women, and we discuss them, and whatever other topics come up."

"What kind of topics?" asked Jeremy.

"Well, the last big one was self-doubt. Do you ever doubt yourself, Jeremy?"

"No, never," he said with a laugh. "But why should that be a topic just for women? I know lots of men with self-doubt, don't you, Max?"

"You're looking at one," said Max. "I question myself all the time. I can't imagine how you can be a decent human being and not question yourself."

"Then your life must be extremely tedious," said Jeremy. "How on earth do you make decisions?"

"When I have a decision to make I talk it over with Sarah," said Anne.

"No you don't," said Sarah. "You do what you want, and then you come to talk to me."

"Do I?" asked Anne. "It seems to me I'm always asking your advice because you're so insightful."

"So what good am I, Anne?" asked Jeremy, laughing.

"Oh, but Jeremy, you're so jolly, and I always want to know what you think about things." Anne's voice trailed off, and she looked extremely uncomfortable. She turned toward Sarah as if to ask her to get her out of the hole she had dug for herself, but Sarah was having none of it.

"Self-doubt is a woman's disease as I've said before, so we'll just make Max an honorary woman," she said.

"Oh no," said Hannah, "don't be ridiculous, Sarah, no one ever really knows what they're doing. And besides, it's time for dinner. So I'll just grab Lucy and ask everyone to sit down. There are place cards."

Lucy went out to the kitchen to get everything out of the oven. She hoped nervously that they had enough food. Hannah followed her, looking put out.

"What does Max mean when he says he doubts himself all the time?" she whispered to Lucy. "Oh, I don't know," whispered Lucy, "Why do you care?"

"Because he's always laying down the law to me about having faith and believing in God, and now he seems to be denying all that." Lucy took the hot fish pans out of the oven and began to put the fish onto plates. She could not believe that Hannah was complaining about Max at her lovely dinner party.

"Oh, just enjoy yourself, Hannah" she whispered, hoping that her annoyance was not too obvious. She went back into the room and said, "If everyone sits down, Hannah will bring in the plates." Everyone did as requested and found themselves with a plate of fish, swimming in white sauce, slightly overdone roast potatoes, and rather crunchy beans.

"I say, this looks delicious," said Charlotte gamely. She now looked very pleased to be sitting next to Adam, who was at the head of the table. Lucy sat at the foot near the door. Hannah finally sat down between Max and Lucy and opposite Jeremy. Max was going around the table filling everyone's glass with a "good white burgundy," looking proud of his knowledge of wine. Now he sat down next to Hannah, and Lucy saw him give her hand a squeeze. Hannah smiled.

There was a lull in the conversation as everyone started to eat. Then Lucy said, "Adam, you've been in England only a short time; tell us how the English are different from the Austrians." Then she immediately thought, "God, what an obvious question; I sound like an interviewer." But Adam came to life and was quite ready to answer her. "Well, the English are decent, and the Austrians are not."

"You mean they are indecent?" Jeremy asked with a provocative look at Sarah, who was sitting next to him.

"Not quite that," replied Adam, "I mean that the Austrians have a boundless creativity and are prepared to examine the depths of the human soul, to live on the edge. Look at all the artists and thinkers who have come from Austria: Mozart, Haydn, and Schubert, and then Freud—and also, of course, Hitler. We have produced the greatest good and the greatest evil. No one is playing by the rules in Austria." Adam looked at Lucy and smiled. Lucy looked at Anne in light of their brief exchange about the Nazis in Austria. She was listening intently to Adam.

"But what about Shakespeare?" asked Charlotte. "Surely Shakespeare trumps everyone?"

"Of course he does," said Max crossly. "And there are so many other great English thinkers; I don't know how you can make a sweeping statement like that, Adam."

Lucy said hastily, "Yes, Shakespeare was certainly plumbing the depths long before Freud, but it is true that, in England, people don't like to acknowledge what's going on inside them."

"Well, so what's going on inside you, Lucy, that you don't want to acknowledge?" asked Jeremy, quick as a flash. Lucy blushed and said, "Well, I suppose I asked for that—nothing of any interest to you at all."

Sarah finished the last of her fish, looked up, and said, "Of course, Freud is very anti-women, treating them as if they simply lack what men have and never get over it. I think the problem is that men are deeply jealous of women because they can't give birth, and they're always worried about the paternity of their children. Children are merely chattels to them; they just want to safeguard their property."

There was silence in the room after this; Sarah was always so forceful. Lucy thought this was not the time for one of Sarah's speeches. Anne looked worried. Lucy saw that she was in a difficult position as both Sarah and Jeremy were her friends. Jeremy was sitting two chairs away from her with Sarah in between so Anne could not see his face, but Lucy observed that he was smiling at his plate in a mocking way, and she felt distinctly uncomfortable.

"Nonsense Sarah," Jeremy said. "Men love their children and want to be fathers, just as women want to be mothers. It has nothing to do with property and everything to do with love. Your world seems to be entirely devoid of human emotion, Sarah, with everyone acting as automatons in pursuit of power. I don't see the world like that at all."

Sarah looked daggers at Jeremy but retreated without replying. Lucy was on Jeremy's side in this interchange, but she was worried about the acrimonious tone the argument had taken.

Hannah stepped in hastily. "Well, I think it's time for dessert," she said. "I'll take your plates, and Lucy can bring it in. No, Max, no need for you to get up at all, there's really no room!" The bustle served to diffuse the tension in the room, and the gateau was produced with a flourish.

"I *say,*" said Charlotte, "that looks *wonderful,* where *did* you get it?"

Max produced a different wine, and everyone ate their cake with relish. "I've just visited Ely Cathedral," he said. "It is absolutely beautiful, with those great grey Norman columns rising to the roof. There is an atmosphere of tremendous peace."

"Oh yes," said Jeremy, "the orchestra played the Verdi Requiem there last year. In the "Dies Irae," the distant trumpets were hidden behind the columns, and when it was their turn to play they moved forward so the people sitting in the nave saw just the shaft of the trumpets but not the players. It was spectacular."

Lucy said, "Well I've never seen Ely nor heard the Verdi Requiem, but I would love to do both."

"Maybe you would like to come to Ely with me?" Adam said to Lucy. "It must be very different from St. Stephen's Cathedral in Vienna with its gothic architecture and baroque ornamentation."

Lucy was overwhelmed by this very public invitation. She blushed and murmured, "How nice," and then distracted herself by offering everyone more cake.

Max looked furious. Lucy was afraid he had taken a real dislike to Adam, and then Jeremy had just upstaged him. It was all very unfortunate. Lucy was beginning to see Max as a grumpy, touchy character with no sense of humor. However, after dinner he lit his pipe and puffed away in a contented manner, so Lucy hoped that the animosity had passed.

Sarah offered cigarettes to everyone, and Jeremy accepted with an ironic look. Hannah produced instant coffee. Lucy was beginning to feel that the party was a success after all. There was a lull in the conversation, so Lucy turned to Jeremy and said in her interview voice, "Jeremy, if you look back on your freshman year, what did you like most about it?"

"Ah," said Jeremy, "now that's a question to be thought about." He drew on his cigarette and blew a few perfect smoke rings, looking surprisingly worldly for one with such a youthful appearance. "I think what I liked most was the women." Everyone laughed. He continued, "This English idea of keeping boys and girls apart in school throughout their childhood and adolescence is for the birds. It was such a relief finally to meet a girl. Well, Lucy, what do you like best about Cambridge in your first year?"

"Oh, same thing: making new friends, both men and women," said Lucy. What she really wanted to say was "falling in love."

"Well, we're certainly not here for the food," said Charlotte. "This dinner excepted, of course." The conversation flowed again as everyone compared notes on food in their colleges and agreed with Somerset Maugham that the best thing to do in England was to eat breakfast three times a day.

Before they knew it, it was 10:30 and the bell rang to alert all guests to leave the college. There was a clattering sound of men's feet running down the stairs. Max, Adam, and Jeremy got up to leave. Adam kissed Lucy's cheek and said, "I'll be in touch," and then he was gone. Max also kissed Hannah on the cheek as he went. Jeremy said to Lucy, "This was a lovely evening. I hope I see you again soon," which Lucy thought a bit odd since she supposed he was with Anne. Everyone else stayed behind to do the washing up and talk. Lucy couldn't believe that her dinner party was over so soon. She had relished being in Adam's presence and, even though they were in a group, she felt she had been the focus of his attention. She was longing to see him again.

9

Interior Castle

The next Thursday morning Lucy, Hannah, and Max were sitting on a bench in the Emmanuel College garden by the pond, looking at the ducks. It was a surprisingly warm day for November, the sun shining through the almost bare branches of the huge trees ranged around them. Hannah and Max leaned against each other as they regarded the ducks contentedly swimming in the pond or waddling on the grass in search of handouts. Lucy stretched out her legs and leaned back as she breathed in the beautiful scene. She and Hannah had been visiting Max to talk about dates for their performing party, and he had suggested that they take advantage of the sunny day and go outside. Max said: "Isn't it ghastly news that President Kennedy has been shot?"

"Yes, we all heard it last night on the radio; it's hard to believe," replied Hannah. "It seems that every time there is a reason for hope in the world it all gets taken away. I'm really sorry for the Americans. The threat of nuclear war with the Russians is such a responsibility."

"Well, ours too," said Max. "We have nuclear submarines too, you know."

"I know," said Hannah, "and I'm against them. I hand it to Sarah. She and her mother have been demonstrating for years against nuclear weapons; they are stalwarts of the Campaign for Nuclear Disarmament and go to all sorts of demonstrations. I should take a leaf out of her book."

"I think you take Sarah far too seriously," said Max.

"What on earth do you mean?" replied Hannah.

"I think Jeremy had it right at the party when he said that Sarah views the world as inhabited by automatons, not people. The way she sees men as simply power-seekers is horrible. I hope that's not how you view me."

"No, of course not," replied Hannah. "But I think it's wrong to dismiss everything Sarah says."

"But I do dismiss it," said Max. "I think she's an immature, obsessive personality whose only way of relating to other people is to harangue them."

"Well, I think she speaks a lot of truth," said Hannah.

Lucy said, "I know what Max means; as Jeremy said at the party, there's no such thing as love in Sarah's world."

Hannah said to Max, "Speaking of truth, where did all this self-doubt that you told everybody about come from? Why did you never tell me about it?"

"Well, I thought you would know," said Max. "Everyone with faith has doubts. That's what faith is: believing beyond doubt. And sometimes the doubt becomes so big you can't seem to get over it."

"So is it true that you have doubts all the time?" asked Hannah.

"Yes, because I think about God all the time, so of course the doubt is always there."

"But isn't that true of life in general?" asked Lucy. "Everything is risky, and we don't know what is going to happen. We could get run over by a bus tomorrow. And look at President Kennedy; all of a sudden everything is changed and no one knows what to do. So we all just struggle along."

"Well, at least I have you," said Max putting his arm around Hannah and giving her a squeeze. "I'll take my chances with the bus." Lucy felt distinctly *de trop*. She was relieved when Hannah got up and said, "I've got so much to do," and pulled Max up with her. She and Lucy left him and went their separate ways. Neither had mentioned to Max that they were due at Sarah's Circle in an hour.

Lucy was the first to arrive in Charlotte's room. They both sat on the floor by the fire waiting for the rest of the Circle to arrive. The fire was bright and hot and Charlotte was, as usual, brewing tea. She couldn't wait to talk about the dinner party with Lucy. "Adam is really dishy, *so* attractive," she said. "I had a long conversation with him about poetry, and Goethe in particular, whom I've only read in translation—and he was very knowledgeable; how did you catch him?"

Lucy was used to Charlotte's outspokenness, but nonetheless she was put out; she couldn't stand the idea that she had somehow "caught" Adam. It made her seem so calculating. So she answered coolly, "Fiona Banks introduced us; we have a mutual friend in Vienna."

"I wish someone would introduce me to a man like that. He really seems to like you."

Lucy was pacified by this observation but she was guarded in her answer: "We don't really know each other very well yet."

"I bet Fiona likes him too," said Charlotte. Lucy looked surprised. "Oh, I don't know," she said, "I think they're just good friends." Charlotte looked hard at Lucy in a pitying way as she re-filled her cup.

Sarah arrived and immediately sat in a chair, which put her above the others sitting on the floor. She said, "That was a really nice party, Lucy. But I didn't like Jeremy at all. I can't imagine what Anne sees in him. He seems so full of himself without having any reason to be."

Lucy and Charlotte exchanged glances. Lucy thought Sarah would certainly not like any man Anne took to; of course she would treat him as a threat. Then again, Jeremy had flatly contradicted her views. But neither of them said a word, and it was just as well, because at that moment Anne arrived with Hannah on her heels. They all sat down, and Charlotte poured the tea. There was a strange silence in the room. Lucy was thinking about Adam and wondering what he had thought about the party and whether he had seen her in a different light after all.

Finally Sarah said, "Well, Lucy, *Interior Castle* was your suggestion, so why don't you tell us what you think about it."

Lucy had guessed that she was going to be put on the spot, so she had made a few notes to which she now referred.

"First, I love St. Teresa's idea that we should give up wanting worldly things like 'possessions, or honors or business,' and seek self-knowledge and humility. Then, I like the thought that we can hear God calling us to discover who we are by going into different rooms of our souls, getting closer and closer to him. I think this is a good description of how one discovers things about oneself; one has to keep crossing thresholds to reach new understanding. Each threshold is difficult; one has to overcome something in oneself that is a barrier to the truth."

Lucy paused and looked around the room to see what effect her words were having on the others. There was silence, so she could not tell.

"What's an example of a threshold?" asked Sarah, breaking the silence.

For a moment, Lucy was at a loss. The threshold she was thinking about had to do with her recognition of the fact that she was in love with Adam. But she certainly wasn't going to say this in front of everyone, especially not Sarah.

Hannah saved her. "I have an example," she said. "I resisted Sarah's point of view about how the patriarchy disadvantages women, but then I realized in orchestra that I was on the second desk when I should be on the first and that there were no other women on a first desk, so I changed my mind and concluded that, in this case, Sarah's view was right. It was like crossing a threshold to new understanding."

Sarah looked gratified by this, but Lucy was worried that Anne would resent the implied criticism of Jeremy. However, Anne was not in the orchestra, so she did not notice. Instead she said, speaking with uncustomary force, "I don't think that's a good example at all. St. Teresa is talking about our resistance toward loving God completely and entirely and overcoming things like pride and self-importance. She says one has to learn how to love others more than ourselves and that learning is difficult. At least that's what I thought she was saying." Anne's voice began to trail away. She automatically looked at Sarah. Sarah obliged.

"St. Teresa is looking for a union with God. But that requires totally giving up the self and humiliating oneself before God, whom she calls 'His Majesty.' I can't see that this applies to anyone but nuns, who have chosen that life. For lay women, obliterating the self is a disaster. Women have been taught for centuries to humiliate themselves before men and to obliterate their sense of self. Feminism is against that. Look at what Simone de Beauvoir has to say about women being in love. Let's see, I wrote down the quote." Sarah was looking in a small notebook. "Here it is: '...destined to the male from childhood, habituated to seeing in him a superb being whom she cannot possibly equal. . . . There is no other way out than to lose herself, body and soul, in him who is represented to her as the absolute, as the essential. . . . She will enthrone him as supreme value and reality; she will humble herself to nothingness before him. Love becomes for her a religion.' This sounds like St. Teresa," she said triumphantly. "St. Teresa has transferred her love for men to God!"

Lucy did not agree with this at all. Even though Adam was all-in-all to her, she believed she had found not lost herself through him. Without him she often felt like nothing, but with him she felt alive.

Hannah spoke. "Well I don't worship Max at all," she said. "He's very solidly human to me; and I don't take his word for everything either. We often argue. So I think de Beauvoir is exaggerating about love. On the other hand, it is true that men often treat women as lesser beings, as in the example of the orchestra."

Charlotte said, "I object to the fact that both these books treat women as pathetic objects needing to be shown the right path by the writer. I think I am fine, I think women are fine, and I object to the idea that I am constantly humiliating myself because I am participating in what Sarah calls the patriarchy. I think women and men are meant to be together, and I'm just looking for an interesting man who likes me as much as I like him. What on earth is wrong with that?"

"Oh, Charlotte," said Sarah, "you just don't understand."

"Well, I suppose Charlotte is entitled to her point of view," said Anne quietly. Sarah looked with complete surprise at Anne; this was a bold contradiction, however gently spoken. Lucy also wondered whether Jeremy had had something to do with Anne's new self-confidence. Then she caught herself; here again she was thinking that you had to have a man to gain confidence. Charlotte said, "Well, thank you Anne, my thoughts exactly."

They seemed to have reached the end of their discussion. Lucy left with her mind spinning. She wanted to be alone to think about what love meant, and where religion fit in. After all, religion was about love if nothing else. Were there two kinds of love, one for people and one for God—or were they the same? Her love for Adam welled up in her heart, and she longed for him in much the same way that she yearned for God. And then she wondered why religion connected love with humility, and if humility was a virtue or a crime against oneself, as Sarah believed.

When she got back to her room she found Jeremy waiting outside her door. She couldn't imagine why he was there, and she could think of no one less welcome now when she wanted to be alone.

"Goodness, Jeremy!" she exclaimed, annoyed. "How long have you been waiting?"

"Oh, just a few minutes," he replied. "I thought I'd stick around on the off-chance."

"Well, do come in," said Lucy, mustering up her good manners and trying to be gracious.

"I just came round to thank you for that lovely party," he said. He looked happy to be let in. "Oh, it was nothing," said Lucy, "I'm glad you could come." She didn't want to offer him anything and so prolong the visit, but she found herself saying, "Would you like a glass of sherry?"

"Oh yes, please," he said. Then looking at Adam's anemones that were now on the mantelpiece, he said, "Those really are very pretty flowers—you don't see them much."

Lucy poured him a glass of sherry and tried to stifle her impatience. "Yes, they are nice, aren't they?"

"This is really good sherry," he said. "Spanish?"

"Yes," said Lucy, "not South African! My mother boycotts South African products because of apartheid, so I have to be careful what I buy."

"You have a laudable mother," said Jeremy. "I wish I did." He stopped, and Lucy wondered what he meant. Then he said, "My mother died when I was twelve and my father sent me off to boarding school, which I enjoyed very much once I got over the initial shock. But I missed my mother for years, still do. Luckily, my father and I are jolly good friends and I always look forward to seeing him during the holidays. He went to my college; Clare too."

"With the fabulous Fellow's garden along the river!" said Lucy. She was moved by Jeremy's story. She could not imagine how one could survive such a loss and then talk about it so calmly. She looked at him more warmly, but did not want to embarrass him by asking any questions. He responded to her sympathetic look by saying, "So, Lucy," observing her intensely, "what is your goal in life?"

"Good heavens!" said Lucy laughing. "That's a big question. I don't think I have one at the moment, except to get my essays written on time. What's your goal?"

"Oh, I just want to keep on doing more science. I'm reading chemistry, you know, and I love it."

"How on earth did you meet Anne? She's doing English, so you couldn't have met in lectures."

"Oh, we met at the freshmen's fair. She and I are both interested in photography, and there's a society for that as there is for every single hobby. We've been seeing each other at meetings, and then she very kindly asked me to your party, so I came. She's a really brilliant photographer."

Still waters run deep, thought Lucy, with a new respect for Anne. Surprisingly, she was enjoying the conversation, so she said, "Would you like another glass?"

"Just a half, I've got to get back in time for dinner."

"I was interested in what Adam said about the Austrians, and plumbing the depths. But they did support Hitler, you know," he continued.

"Well, Adam's about five years older than I, so he was a child in the war and can't be said to have been involved, can he?" asked Lucy, wondering how Jeremy could be so nice and so provocative at the same time.

"Oh no, I wasn't suggesting that he was," he said, looking at his watch. "I'd really better be going now. It's been jolly nice talking to you, and thanks again for the wonderful party." He took himself off, and Lucy finally had time to reflect. She looked out of the window. Autumn was reaching its end, and winter and Christmas would soon be here. The gardens were covered in yellow and brown leaves, and the gardeners were at work with their rakes. Jeremy had asked what her goal in life was. She knew it was to be with Adam.

Later, after dinner, she made one of her regular trips to the post boxes. There she found a note from Adam. It read:

Dear Lucy,

Come to Ely with me next Sunday. If we catch the early train we can be in time for the morning service at eleven. Thank you for the wonderful dinner.

Adam

10

Ely

Lucy woke the next day in a happy mood. She felt sure the visit to Ely would be the defining moment in her relationship with Adam. He would not have invited her to spend the day with him and visit Ely Cathedral if he did not care for her. She dressed carefully but did not put her hair up because she did not think it would last the whole day. So she combed it thoroughly and put on a little makeup. Her coat, the same one she had worn in Vienna, was not elegant, but it would have to do.

Their rendezvous was at the station; it was raining hard. Lucy was there ten minutes before the time and stood outside under her umbrella looking anxiously for Adam. With relief she saw him get off the next bus. "Quick, inside, you silly girl!" he said, and taking her arm propelled her into the station. They shook themselves like dogs and laughed at each other. "Come on," said Adam, "we've just got time for a quick coffee."

"This is not like a Viennese *mélange*," complained Lucy as they sipped the watery brew, "but it is nice and hot." Adam nodded and smiled. "I'm really glad to be here with you," he said. Lucy glowed. Then he produced a guide to Ely Cathedral and started showing her some of the pictures and reading to her from the guide book. "Oh, not yet," she protested, "I want to see it with completely fresh eyes."

"All right then, I'll just get a paper and we can read it on the train." He ran to the kiosk on the platform and returned with the *Times*. On the train, they sat together in a crowded compartment.

"Why are so many people all going to Ely on a Sunday?" whispered Lucy.

"Perhaps they have the same idea as we," Adam whispered back. "We might as well read. Would you like the front page or the opinions?"

"The opinions," said Lucy. "I know I shouldn't, but I like people to tell me what I ought to be thinking about politics. Then I can decide more easily whether I agree or not."

"Aren't you interested in politics then?" asked Adam.

"I was brought up with socialism, and I hate injustice of any kind, but I'm not politically active at all," she replied. "When I was six, I was. I remember carrying a lot of bright orange 'VOTE LABOUR' posters for people to put in their front windows. I was extremely proud of myself."

Lucy waited for Adam to declare his politics, but he didn't; he just began reading his part of the paper, and there was silence between them until the train drew into Ely. The rain had stopped and there was a weak sun, but the air was cold.

They wandered together through the little town of Ely. Lucy had seen many a medieval village before, but this was the most beautiful. It seemed unchanged from the past, and even the few shops looked ancient. They approached the cathedral from the west side along a leafy path. They walked around it so that they could see the great tower with its belfry and turrets rising above them, the transepts and the octagon. They stood for a while and gazed at the cathedral through the misty air, and Lucy thought that it was well named the "Ship of the Fens." Finally, feeling the cold, they went in through the big arched doorway and stood just inside looking down the long nave to the octagon and the filigreed wooden altar. On either side, the tall grey Norman arches rose to a great height. A magnificent Victorian painted ceiling hid the rafters above. It was breathtaking, and Lucy stood in awe. Adam took Lucy's hand as they walked slowly down the nave and, although they were both silent, Lucy felt sure that a great love was growing between them. The service was not to begin for another half hour; a few other people were walking slowly around and looking at all the treasures. "Religion must be right," said Lucy. "I feel such peace here. To think that this has been a sacred space for over a thousand years! Think about what a vision of God it took to build it. And to be able to make the vision live through stone; think of the masons and the stone carvers they must have needed. Surely each one was inspired by God, or it wouldn't be so perfect."

"You *are* a socialist at heart, Lucy," said Adam, laughing and breaking the spell, "always thinking about the workers!"

They wandered down the nave and looked up at the high octagon with its beautiful paintings and stained glass window. The altar was being made ready for the service, so they walked back to the chairs set out in the nave. Lucy knelt to say a prayer. She usually felt so far from God she started her prayer like a letter: "Dear God." Then she never knew what else to say, so she often just said the Lord's Prayer. But this time she knew, and she prayed, "Thank you for bringing me here with Adam." Adam was also kneeling beside her. She wondered what he was thinking and if he had a special route to God.

The service of Morning Prayer began. Lucy loved the liturgy and the hymns with their great harmonies and stirring words. Her favorite was "Love divine, all loves excelling," but it was not sung this morning. The choir did sing a spectacular Mozart anthem, "Splendente Te," which sounded like something out of an opera. Lucy was in heaven. She almost felt she was marrying Adam and that the whole service was a celebration of their love. They stood for the final hymn as the choir paraded out and then walked slowly outside with the rest of the congregation.

It had begun to rain again, so they did not linger. Instead, they walked quickly to a little restaurant that they had spotted on their way in. They sat at a small round table and ordered soup and rolls. Lucy felt light with happiness. Surely this was love, she thought, and surely he felt it too; he must. The experience in the cathedral had been too intense for him not to be moved. She was sure he loved her.

"How did you enjoy *Interior Castle*?" he asked.

"I loved it," said Lucy. "I loved the terrible animals and reptiles in the first room, who try to deter you from moving forward. I have so many voices in my head that tell me I'm no good, and never will find God; they're just like those reptiles—negative voices talking and talking to me. And then I loved the description of periods of 'aridity.' Just when you think you've found God, you lose your confidence again and have no feeling at all. That phase seems to go on forever. Then St. Teresa's happiness at finding God in the last room is palpable, and the idea that she can never lose Him again. I don't suppose I'll ever be free of doubts about God, but I do believe in the power of love to transform you. That's how I feel now; I feel transformed." She looked at him with a frank gaze.

"These are profound thoughts," he said after a while. "I'll never forget them."

For Lucy, Adam's words confirmed her in her love for him. It was right that she loved him, just as it was right to love God. It never occurred to her that Adam did not feel as she did in that moment.

When they got up to leave, Adam helped her on with her coat. Turning her toward him, he buttoned her coat for her and then kissed her gently on the lips. "You are wonderful," he said. They ran back through the streets of Ely to catch their train, holding hands.

As Lucy went down to dinner that night after checking her post by the Porter's lodge, she glanced outside and saw a group of Oldwick students and a few men about to enter the college. It was dark and she could not see them clearly, but she suddenly thought she caught a glimpse of Adam among them. Surely it was he; yes, she recognized his face, the cast of his jaw, and the coat he had on earlier in Ely. She peered out into the dark and made out Jane and Camilla among the group, and there was Fiona. Lucy saw her jostle her way close to Adam, looking up at him and laughing in her flirtatious way. Suddenly she saw Fiona take Adam's hand as the group moved toward the front doors. Adam did not resist. He let himself be pulled toward the entrance to the college, and he was laughing too.

Lucy fled back to her room. Dinner was now impossible; she couldn't bear to be with other people. She couldn't imagine how Adam could dream of going out with Fiona and her friends after their lovely day at Ely. Their day had been solemn and true, and full of love. Their relationship had been blessed in the Cathedral. And now Adam was already with Fiona. Lucy lay on her bed and cried.

The next morning she awoke thinking about Ely. Her love for Adam flowed through her again, coming up from the depths of her being like a great river of shining water. Then the image of him with Fiona intruded, but she found herself pushing it away. She knew in her heart that her experience with Adam had been unique. Fiona was far too small a person to destroy it, she thought. Her mood lifted and the day looked brighter.

11

The Playing Party

The Black Dog was a little pub down a lane in the middle of Cambridge. At six in the evening, the pub was full of men, mainly undergraduates drinking beer, and very noisy. A good coal fire was burning in an enormous fireplace and, in the far corner, a game of darts elicited cheers and laughter. The tables in a dimly lit space in the rear of the pub were also full, each with two or three older, better dressed men talking together. Sarah, Lucy, and Anne sat at one of these tables. Extremely self-conscious, Anne bit her fingernails and kept her eyes on her shandy. Sarah, by contrast, had a defiant air, stared straight back at the many men who were staring at her, and sipped her bitter ale as if it were the nectar of the gods.

"Girls don't go to pubs alone," Anne had protested when Sarah had suggested it.

"I know," said Sarah, "but there's no law against it, and it's good to challenge the status quo. Why should men have all the fun? Every man I know is in a pub at least twice a week if not more often. We're just stuck with sherry in our rooms. Why can't we get out and about as men do?"

So Anne had allowed herself to be taken to the Black Dog but had insisted that Lucy come as well. Lucy had reluctantly agreed. She had never been inside a pub before and wanted to know what it was like. They had immediately attracted stares, and the barman asked them sardonically, "What will it be, ladies?" But they had remained cool and given their order, and here they were discussing Charlotte.

"I don't know why I wanted her in the Circle," said Sarah. "She contradicts everything I say about the predicament of women and seems awfully interested in finding a man. Did you see how she positioned herself right next to Adam when she came in? She just went straight for him. Didn't you mind, Lucy?"

Lucy remembered that she had been decidedly disappointed that she had not had the chance of a single word with Adam before Charlotte arrived, but she said, "Of course not, why should I mind? Who am I to say with whom Adam should talk? The whole idea of the dinner party is that everyone talks to everyone else. And Charlotte has a lot to say."

"Charlotte may not agree with you," said Anne to Sarah, "but I think she's very interested in the books we read and the topics we discuss. If she weren't, she wouldn't come to the Circle."

"I suppose that's true," said Sarah. "I do like Charlotte's down-to-earth manner; she's certainly completely honest and doesn't give herself airs. And speaking of men," she continued, "how are you getting on with Jeremy, Anne?"

"Really, Sarah," said Anne blushing, "for one so concerned about women's issues, you seem to be remarkably interested in men."

"I'm not, really," said Sarah, "it's just that I saw him leave Lucy's room the other day—just the day after the party, I think it was. I didn't know you were friends with Jeremy, Lucy. I thought you met for the first time when Anne introduced him. I thought none of us knew Anne was bringing him." Sarah sat back in her seat blowing cigarette smoke over them. Lucy thought her pixie face looked even sharper and that she had a self-satisfied smirk. Anne appeared upset by Sarah's innuendo, and Lucy was furious. It was dreadful that Sarah wanted to burst Anne's bubble by implying that she and Jeremy had something going on. She said hastily, "Oh, Jeremy just came to thank me for the party, which was the first time I met him. He stayed just five minutes—that was all."

"Well, that was nice of Jeremy," said Anne. "He's a very thoughtful person." But she shot Sarah an angry glance. Lucy immediately felt guilty that she had allowed Jeremy to stay much longer than the five minutes she had confessed to and had let him to confide in her. But she was even more disturbed by Sarah's schadenfreude. Lucy thought she was jealous of anyone, especially a man, who took Anne's attention away from her. And Jeremy had referred to the Circle as Anne's, which must have increased Sarah's dislike of him. Lucy concluded that Sarah had not, in fact, enjoyed the dinner party very much; she had simply felt left out. But that was no excuse for meanness.

Anne's face was flushed, and she even looked angry. So Lucy was not surprised when she got up, declared that it was time for dinner, grabbed her coat, and left the pub before Sarah could say a word. Lucy and Sarah remained for a while with absolutely nothing to say to each other.

At dinner that night Lucy had put her hair up and was wearing lipstick. The meal was ham and mashed potatoes and those mushy peas, but there was always the hope of a good dessert. Anne, who was sitting with her, said, "Lucy, you're looking so spiffy, are you off to something tonight?"

"Oh no," said Lucy, "only a quartet rehearsal. I'm in such a good mood; I just thought I'd get out of my old clothes for a change. By the way, I've been meaning to tell you: When Jeremy came round to thank me for the party, he said you were a terrific photographer. Have you been doing it for long?"

"Yes, ages," said Anne, "ever since my parents gave me a Brownie camera when I was thirteen. In fact, I entered one of my photos into the *Girl* magazine photo competition, and it won second place."

The desert was jam roly-poly and custard, which Lucy found most delicious. Lucy left before grace, after bowing to the Principal, and ran to her room to pick up her cello. She wanted to be early since it took her so long to tune.

When she reached the rehearsal room she found a note on the door that said, "Hannah will be a few minutes late, start without me." Inside there was no one yet, so she got out her cello, put up her music stand, and tuned. She began to practice the third movement. They were planning to rehearse the whole quartet tonight in preparation for the Christmas playing party that Fiona was organizing. They would invite their friends, and Lucy had suggested they serve madeira wine with madeira cake to go with it—very nineteenth century, she thought.

Next, surprisingly, Fiona arrived looking wonderful. Her thick blond hair had been tamed and coifed; she was wearing lipstick and a black dress with a full skirt. She had pinned an intriguing brooch on her breast. She greeted Lucy with enthusiasm. "Hello Lucy," she said. "Look, aren't you proud of me? I'm not late!"

"Well done," said Lucy, laughing, but not wanting to give her the satisfaction of sounding too impressed. "Was the dinner that good?" asked Max coming in. "You both look so cheerful."

"Oh no," said Lucy, "I'm just happy to be here and am looking forward to getting ready for the playing party."

"Quite," said Max. "Well then, let's begin without Hannah; I'm sure she'll be here in a minute."

Fiona raised her violin and they were off at a good tempo. Lucy was amazed at how well Fiona was playing. She seemed to have a whole new approach to the music, and she didn't stumble in any of the difficult passages. She must have practiced a lot, thought Lucy.

After Hannah arrived, they rehearsed for an hour and a half more. At the end, as they were putting away their instruments, Fiona said, "So where shall we have our playing party? We don't have rooms big enough at Oldwick."

"Come to my rooms," said Max, "I have a large sitting room, and if we don't invite too many people we can surely fit everyone in."

"Would you really lend your room, Max? That's wonderful," said Fiona, "and I promise I won't invite too many, just Adam and Jane and Camilla and maybe two or three more."

At the mention of Adam, Lucy felt a sharp pain. She had hoped to invite him herself, especially now that she imagined they had cemented their special relationship. But then she recalled the glimpse she had had of Fiona pulling Adam by the hand into the college, and her heart sank.

"Who do you want to invite?" asked Fiona, in a patronizing tone.

"I don't know," said Lucy quietly, "I suppose Anne and Charlotte would like to come; I don't know whether Sarah would."

"Max and I have a few friends, don't we Max? We could see if some of them want to come, and I suppose we'll have to ask Jeremy or he'll feel left out."

"That's just about as many as the room will fit," said Max. "Well, it's late and they'll be ringing the bell soon. Will you see me out, Hannah?" As they left, Lucy saw Max take Hannah's hand. She envied them. They were so solid together, and seemed so happy. But then she thought, "What I have with Adam is grand and beautiful. In time we'll be a solid couple too." She remembered his tender kiss as he buttoned her coat and was reassured.

Fiona and Lucy were left in the room together, putting the chairs back in their places and collecting their things.

"Would you like to come to my room for some cocoa?" asked Fiona.

"Oh, I'm sorry, I shouldn't," said Lucy. "My tutorial is tomorrow and I've got to finish my essay."

"Oh, do come," said Fiona, "there's so much to talk about, it would be lovely if you did."

But the last thing Lucy wanted to do was talk about Adam with Fiona, and she was sure that's what Fiona wanted. So she said, "Thank you, but I really can't."

She took herself back to her room, made herself a mug of cocoa, and went into a reverie.

LLL

The next day Lucy was walking along Kings Parade thinking about Adam and Ely. She felt like going into the Kings College chapel and sitting there for a while to recapture her experience at Ely Cathedral in another monumental space. Just as she had reached the entrance to the college, she heard her name called and, looking round, she saw the gnome waving at her. He came running across the road toward her. "Hello, love," he said, "fancy meeting you here."

"Oh Danny, I'm so glad to see you. What are you doing here?" asked Lucy.

"I might ask the same about you," he laughed, "hanging out by a men's college."

"Well, I was just going into the chapel, but I'd much rather have coffee with you," she said, "do you have time?" Lucy was taken aback by her own boldness. She realized that she really wanted to talk to him.

"For you, I always have time," said Danny.

She looked at him anew; his face was still glowing with good cheer. The Copper Kettle was a few paces down the street. They walked there in silence. When they were sitting with their coffee, Danny looked at her and asked, "Is there something on your mind?"

Lucy said, "Well, yes, but I don't know how to tell you about it. It all seems so muddled up."

"That sounds like life," said Danny."It's very hard to be clear about things because they're always changing."

"Oh yes," said Lucy. "I've got two friends, and Sarah has just upset Anne. She implied that Anne's friend was interested in me, and it's really not true. But Anne was very put out, and now I don't know how to approach either. It's all very silly, I know."

"Ah," said Danny, "The green-eyed monster."

"What do you mean?" asked Lucy. "I really don't think Anne is jealous of me, I just think she's upset because Sarah was implying that she had reason to be."

"Oh no," said Danny, "not Anne, Sarah."

"But who is Sarah jealous of? It can't be me, and Anne has always been her pet."

"You'd be surprised how jealous a queen can get when her maid likes someone better than she."

"Oh," said Lucy. "Do you really mean Sarah is jealous of Anne?

"Well, they're your friends and you know them; what do you think?"

"I never thought of that," said Lucy. "How does one get over jealousy, I wonder?"

"Jealous people have been killing their rivals for centuries. Or they kill the betrayer; look at Othello," said Danny.

"But that's not people like us," said Lucy.

"You'd be surprised," said Danny in an ominous voice. Lucy didn't know whether to take him seriously or not, but then she smiled at him and finally laughed.

"Well thanks, Danny," she said, "I'll have to think about all this."

"Just be yourself, love," he said. "You're a nice girl who's been properly brought up; you won't go wrong." Lucy wished she could believe him.

LLL

The playing party took place the next Sunday afternoon. Lucy was waiting for Anne, whom she had asked to carry the cake as Lucy was encumbered with her cello. Anne was late. The quartet had allowed themselves only thirty minutes for a warm-up, and she and Anne still had to get across Cambridge to Max's rooms. While she fumed she looked at herself in the mirror. She had chosen to wear a flowered, light-wool full skirt and a white blouse. Her hair was washed and done up in the familiar chignon. She had put on makeup and lipstick and thought she looked very nice. She hoped Adam would be impressed. Finally Anne arrived wearing one of her dresses, and they could go.

They found Max getting things ready. His room was large, with a good view onto the court. Four chairs for the quartet were arranged in the window, and he had set up more chairs and his two sofas in three rows facing them. The fire was lit on the side wall and the desk was pushed to the back to be used as a table for the wine and cake. Lucy said, "Oh, I hope we're not late, Max." Then she surveyed the room. "Gosh, you've done all the work already. You're so well organized. It looks wonderful." Anne deposited the cake on the table and Max took a peek. "Delicious," he said, "but we'd better leave it in the box until we serve it after we play."

When Hannah arrived, Max said, "You're looking very glamorous." Hannah laughed, "Oh, I don't think so—that word should be reserved for Fiona."

At that moment, Fiona arrived, wearing yet another dress. This one was bright red, with a low-cut collar. It would have looked quite formal if not for the color. She wore a gold necklace and red shoes. She looked stunning and was glowing. Max and Hannah looked at each other and smiled. They all congratulated each other on their looks, particularly Fiona's dress, and Max's bow tie, which Jeremy had showed him how to tie. Max displayed his wine table and pointed proudly to the bottles he had uncorked to let them breathe. The cake was placed next to the wine for cutting after the concert.

Anne settled herself on one of the sofas, and the rest of them played through most of the quartet. When they had finished they left their instruments on the chairs and prepared to greet the guests. Lucy was nervous. She hadn't seen Adam since the day at Ely, almost a week ago. She didn't know why he hadn't come to see her after their wonderful day together and was disappointed that she would meet him again in the middle of so many people. She dressed up specially for him but knew she would be eclipsed by Fiona, who was looking even more beautiful than ever.

In the event, so many people came in at once that she didn't even see Adam enter until it was time to play. She surveyed the audience. Jeremy was sitting with Anne on a sofa, while Jane and Camilla were giggling together, as they always did. They were like school girls, she thought. She couldn't see Adam. Oh, how she hoped he would not be late! Suddenly she saw him in the back row and was just about to give him a wave when Charlotte plonked herself next to him. As he turned toward Charlotte she was just able to see his handsome profile.

The quartet played, and Mozart's music filled the room. The long connecting phrases, the rise and fall of the sound felt to her like breathing a heavenly scent. All the players were breathing as one in the music. At one point she glanced at Adam and saw him looking intently at her. She smiled faintly at him, whereupon he answered her with a brief smile and nod. In the slow movement, as Hannah played the melody, she felt they were all transformed into one instrument. They played the finale passionately—fast and furious. They were greeted with tremendous applause. They stood up, bowed, and sat down again. Jeremy was shouting "Bravo!" The applause swelled again, and they took another bow. Then they looked at each other and laughed with pleasure. They had pulled it off!

Max said, "The wine is open—please help yourselves. Lucy will be serving cake in just a moment." The instruments were put away, and Lucy made her way to the back of the room to open the cake box. As she passed Jeremy and Anne, Jeremy said, "That was wonderful playing, Lucy, such a full, round tone." Lucy thought of Professor Pracht and wished he could have heard her. She reached the back of the room to find Adam, but Fiona was ahead of her. They were talking and laughing. When Adam saw Lucy he abruptly left Fiona and came over to her. "I felt as if I were in Vienna," he said.

"I felt it too," replied Lucy, longing to kiss him. He made no move toward her, but Lucy, laughing and feeling quite giddy, said "Come and help me deal with the cake." He followed her to the table, where they cut the cake and started handing it out on little plates. When Adam got to Fiona, she took her plate and ostentatiously put some cake in her mouth and started to chew it while looking him in the eye. He laughed as she broke off a piece for him and put it in his mouth. Lucy was mortified. He looked around, saw Lucy watching them, and immediately left Fiona. As he moved away he wiped the cake crumbs from his mouth with a perfect white handkerchief.

The party seemed to go on for hours. Jeremy and Anne were giggling a lot like two small children who had been let out to play. Lucy had never seen Anne looking so happy. Max and Hannah were sitting on a sofa. In a daring gesture, Hannah laid her head on Max's shoulder; Max sat very still and cool-looking, as if they did this all the time. Fiona and Adam were talking together again. But Lucy thought of Ely and her own ecstatic experience and dismissed Fiona. She can flirt with Adam all she likes, thought Lucy, but she will never have what I have.

She wearied of all the compliments and talk. Finally, at about 5:00, people began to drift away, everyone warmed and full from the wine and cake. Jeremy said to Anne in a slurry voice, "Would you like me to walk you back to Oldwick? It's already dark. And then you can show me some of your latest photos."

"Oh yes," said Anne with mock formality, "that would be so kind of you." They left arm-in-arm.

Lucy, Max, and Hannah were putting away the chairs and moving the sofas back to where they belonged. Fiona was still talking to Adam. At last, Lucy allowed herself to feel jealous.

"Why does she monopolize him like that?" she thought, "It's so irritating." She was hoping to walk back with Adam, at least until they reached King's. Adam said goodbye to Fiona and came over to her.

"I've got to go to the library," he said, "so I'll have to say goodbye now. This was a wonderful afternoon . . . thank you." He touched her arm and was gone.

Hannah was going to stay behind with Max; he was taking her out to dinner. So Lucy and Fiona found themselves walking home together. The evening was damp and cold with a biting wind. They were each in their own thoughts and found they had nothing to say to each other. Finally, Fiona said, "I'm really glad Adam heard us play, I think he was very impressed." But Lucy was not to be drawn in, and silence returned. At times Fiona seemed to be on the brink of saying something, but then she stopped herself; Lucy did not ask what she wanted to say.

They reached Oldwick and parted. Lucy went back to her own room and lay on the bed. Term was almost over, and the Christmas vacation loomed ahead. How was she going to live without seeing Adam? She would have to be content with writing to him and hoping that he'd respond. Her thoughts went round and round in her head and she fell asleep.

She dreamed she saw a woman kissing Adam in a large and spacious room in some dream house. She realized that she was the woman. Gradually the room became almost dark. Now she was lying on a bed observing him; the woman Adam was still kissing had changed into Fiona.

12

The End of Term

It was the beginning of December, and Lucy was putting up Christmas decorations in her room. She would not be able to admire them for long because the Michaelmas term was over well before Christmas, but she felt in a festive mood. She was making paper chains in the way her family had always done at home. They would put sprigs of holly on the pictures and make a banner out of red crepe paper saying "Merry Christmas" that was hung in the hall to greet people as they came in through the front door. Suddenly Hannah burst into the room and, flopping down on the bed, burst out, "At last Max has kissed me, and we've just spent the last hour kissing."

"Goodness," said Lucy laughing, "You seem so excited; was this really the first time?"

"Yes, and it was so wonderful," said Hannah. "Max came in with some mistletoe and held it above me and just kissed me and then we couldn't stop. I never thought he felt that passionately about me, but he does. I can't believe it, I can't believe it." Hannah sounded very passionate herself. Lucy looked at her again and saw her flushed face; her lips were red and blotchy and her hair was in a terrible mess. But she looked triumphant.

Lucy was seized with a moment of jealousy. She hadn't seen Adam at all after the playing party. Her happiness was sustained only by that one passionate kiss in Botolph's Lane, and here were Hannah and Max, to her mind a very unromantic couple, doing everything she wanted to do with Adam. She said, "Here, help me with these paper chains. I've got some holly; we can stick these sprigs on those pictures of Vienna. Come on Hannah, stop dreaming. You do the holly. And now I want to hear about the whole thing."

Hannah got off the bed, pushed her hair out of her eyes, and spoke urgently as if her life depended on what she said. "When Max first came in, he had a funny look on his face, and was holding something behind his back. He said he had brought me a present, and I couldn't imagine what it could be. Then he produced the mistletoe with a flourish and said he had been thinking about kissing me all day and now he was going to do it. So I just laughed, but then he did start kissing me. And when he finally stopped he said, 'Oh what a brave boy am I!'"

"Well, he certainly was," said Lucy.

"Yes, wasn't he?" said Hannah. "So then we kissed some more and I said, 'Let's sit down,' and then he said 'Let's put our feet up.' And so there we were on the bed just kissing like mad. And in between we had a lovely chat about all our friends. We decided that Sarah would never be interested in any man, and we thought that Jeremy likes you more than Anne."

"Oh no!" Lucy protested, "of course he doesn't, what on earth gave you that idea?"

"I saw the way he was looking at you while we played."

"That's ridiculous," said Lucy. "How could you look at Jeremy and play at the same time?"

"Time will tell," said Hannah.

"So what else?" asked Lucy.

"Well, Max suddenly said, 'Do you think God approves of sex?' I mean can you believe it, he was still thinking about God after all that kissing? So typical!"

"What did you say?" asked Lucy

"I said I thought that sex was love, so of course God approves."

"Are you going to see Max over the vacation?" Lucy asked.

"Oh, I do hope so; the Christmas vac seems so long. Maybe he could come to Manchester and visit my family. I know everyone would love to meet him. What are you going to do?"

"I've no idea. I expect Adam will return to Vienna, so I'll just be at home. I'll probably volunteer in the local secondhand bookshop." Just to see what it sounded like, she spoke of Adam as if their connection were open and solid, as if everyone knew they were together. In fact she had no idea how Adam really felt about her. But in her fantasies they were always together and the Christmas vacation was just a small hiatus in the course of their love for each other. She wished she could confide her real thoughts and feelings to Hannah, but the only thing to tell was her own undying love for Adam, and somehow she just couldn't talk about it, even though Hannah had been so frank with her. When she thought about it, she really had nothing to tell; one kiss, that was all.

When Lucy and Hannah went down to dinner that evening they saw Sarah. Lucy thought she seemed downcast, so when, after dinner, she invited them back to her room, it seemed only charitable to agree to go with her.

Sarah didn't decorate her room at all. "It's all just fake religion," she said. But she lit a few red candles, and the whole room glowed.

"I'm concerned about the circle," she said. "Everybody seems to be losing interest; they're more interested in men than in the 'woman problem.'"

"Oh no," said Lucy, "It's just that we've been so taken up with music we haven't had time for anything else, what with work and so on." In fact, Lucy had not been thinking about the circle at all and had not missed the challenge that it always presented to her. Lucy smiled to herself as she thought that if Sarah knew about Hannah and Max kissing it would drive her to despair. Sarah continued, "There seems to be this idea that if you just get married you'll find immediate, lasting happiness. And that's so wrong. I mean, what are we getting an education for if we're not going to use it for something other than looking after children? That sounds so boring to me. And how many women are doctors and lawyers? Very few! As for business, I can't think of a single woman in this college who wants to go into business. What is wrong with all this?"

Hannah replied, "But if you work, who looks after the children? I would hate to leave my children with a nanny; it would be a terrible abdication of responsibility."

"Oh, lots of families have nannies," said Sarah, who had evidently never thought about having children with anybody. "It's just the working-class women who can't afford them. And there are no public nurseries available for them. So all the women are stuck at home while their husbands go out and have interesting lives."

"You know, it is strange that we talk about the 'woman problem' as if everything is the fault of women. But that doesn't explain why women don't talk about the man problem," said Hannah. "I wonder why they don't?"

"Oh, come on," said Sarah, "we all know the answer to that." Sarah was back to her main theme. "The whole society is dominated by men. Why should they want to give up their power?"

Lucy said, "Power seems like such an empty thing to me, I can't imagine wanting to have power over anyone." As she said this she reflected that, after all, Adam had great power over her. He could change her life in a moment by loving her or not.

"That's just your religion talking," said Sarah, "all that emphasis on humility."

"But what about love?" asked Lucy. "Why can't men and women be partners?"

"We've had this conversation so many times before," said Sarah, "and no one is changing their opinion."

"Well, you certainly aren't," said Hannah. "You just don't see any good in men at all, and we're not in that camp, are we Lucy?"

"No," said Lucy faintly, but was not inclined to say more.

"And it's not true that I haven't changed my opinion," said Hannah. "I've become much more aware of how much men dominate us, thanks to you, Sarah."

Sarah looked gratified by this remark, and the tension in the room lessened.

"This discussion has been good," she said, like a teacher praising her pupils. "Maybe the Circle is not quite dead yet."

Lucy marveled that Sarah was fed by such a discussion. She suddenly realized that Sarah needed them and felt a surge of compassion for her. Her irritation disappeared. It must be lonely to be a prophet crying in the wilderness with nobody taking you seriously. Of course, Anne had been a disciple rather than a friend, someone who would listen to her and agree. That's what Sarah needed around her: disciples who would boost her up. And that's what she wanted Lucy to be and what Lucy wouldn't be. She could not even say that she took Sarah very seriously. She just thought her view was narrow and that she hadn't experienced life as Lucy had. But she respected Sarah's energy and conviction.

Later that evening Jeremy walked into her room and announced, "I've brought you a present for Christmas."

"My goodness," said Lucy, "this is much too much, I mean, how kind of you." She did not really want to see Jeremy now and was puzzled by his visit.

"Do open it now," he said.

It was a book containing color reproductions of Klimt's *Beethoven Frieze*, which Lucy had seen and admired in the Secession building in Vienna. Lucy was stunned and thrilled.

"How on earth did you know that I liked these paintings?" she gasped, "and how did you find this book?"

"I was in the bookshop, and your friend Adam walked in. He recognized me and we had a chat. This book was displayed among the art books, and I saw him looking at it. He mentioned that the original was in Vienna and I immediately thought it was something that you might like, so I just snapped it up. And here it is!" Jeremy was triumphant.

Lucy was mortified. Why couldn't it have been Adam who gave her the book? Then she would treasure it forever. But it was Jeremy who had thought of her, and while she couldn't imagine why he wanted to give her a present in the first place, her basic politeness took over; she thanked him, invited him to sit down, and offered him some cocoa. She was annoyed all over again when he accepted.

"My father lives in London, like your family," he said. He must have had this information from Anne. "So I was hoping we could meet during the Christmas vac. We could go to the cinema or something."

Lucy wondered what was going on. Now he was actually inviting her out with no thought of Anne. Maybe Hannah and Max were right that he really liked her. But she dismissed the thought immediately. Anne was Jeremy's friend, and Lucy did not want in any way to be a rival.

"Oh, that would be nice," she said vaguely, just wishing that he would leave her alone.

They chatted on about their plans for the Christmas vacation, and then Jeremy took out his address book and asked for her telephone number. Reluctantly, she complied. Maybe she could put him off later. Luckily, as soon as he had put his little book away he got up and said he had to leave, as he was going home the next morning and had all his packing to do. He took himself off, whistling as he went.

Lucy was due to leave in two days. She was worried that she had not heard from Adam at all and did not know whether it was appropriate for her to go to see him in his rooms. Her longing overwhelmed her prudence, and the next morning she got on her bike and cycled over to King's. Adam was packing; clothes and books were strewn round the room. A little alarm shook her with the thought that perhaps he had intended to leave without saying good-bye.

As if reading her mind, he said, "Oh, Lucy, I'm so glad to see you. I was going to walk over to Oldwick this afternoon to say good-bye. I'm off to Vienna tomorrow. Please forgive the mess. Just let me move this stuff and you can sit here," he said pointing to a chair by the fire. Lucy sat down and looked at him. She was bursting with love for him and longing for him to embrace her and let her know how much he would miss her. She said in a constricted voice, "I'm going home soon too. I hope you have a wonderful time at home in Vienna. I wish I were going with you." She couldn't believe herself; how could she blurt out such a thing? But Adam just smiled and said kindly, "That would be nice; but I'll be back next term and we can see each other again then." Then he sat on the arm of her chair and put his arm round her. "You'll be very glad to see your family," he said. "It's good to go home." Lucy held back tears. "I suppose so," she said. Adam seemed not to notice that anything was wrong. He gave her a squeeze, got up, and said firmly, "Now you must go and let me finish my packing. I'll write to you from Vienna and tell you about the food!" Lucy managed a smile as she too got up and walked slowly toward the door. They stood facing each other, and Adam bent down and kissed her cheek. "I won't forget Ely," he said. She smiled at him, and he looked approvingly at her as if he thought how easy she was to please.

But Lucy was not pleased. As she ran down the stairs the tears began to flow, and for the first time that term she started to long for home.

Part II

Christmas and Lent Term

13

Jeremy

Home felt like a sanctuary. Lucy had been so eager to leave it and spread her wings in Vienna and Cambridge, and now she was glad to be back. The modest house in a leafy suburb of South London on the edge of Greenwich Park, tea with the family in the living room with the coal-burning stove, the kitchen table over which confidences were exchanged among the women—all these things were like a balm to Lucy's soul and regenerated her strength. Her parents welcomed her warmly. Mr. Page was interested in her studies at Cambridge, and her mother was so excited by Lucy's return that she stopped worrying and was simply affectionate and sweet. Usually Lucy did not feel particularly close to Anthea, who was so different from her, matter of fact and down to earth, rather like Charlotte. But now she and Anthea greeted each other with affection. Her family did not seem to notice that she had changed at all, but she did not mind. She was just glad to be at home where she did not have to try, to yearn, to deal with difficult feelings. Home was familiar and very restful.

One day, as they walked in the afternoon in the park, Lucy told her mother and sister about Adam. "I really like him," she said, "but I don't know whether he likes me or not."

"Well, why not ask him?" said Anthea.

"It never occurred to me to do so," she replied. "I just assumed he would say something if he wanted to."

"How passive can you be?" said Anthea. "You mean you've been seeing him the whole term long and never asked him what he felt about you? You just waited to see what would happen? You're just taking your cues from him; you're doing whatever he wants, and you're not saying anything about what you want. He's just controlling you, and you're letting him. That's so unliberated."

Lucy was shocked and chastened. At first she was angry that Anthea had spoken to her in this blunt way, seemingly without sympathy for her.

But then she thought that Anthea could have a point. It was true that Adam had been totally unforthcoming about his feelings for her, and she wondered about Fiona. But she put these thoughts away and dwelt only on the kiss and the experience at Ely. It did not seem to her that being in love meant you were a victim; Anthea simply didn't understand. She waited every day for a letter from Adam but none came. Other letters did. Hannah wrote:

Dear Lucy,

It is so strange to be at home again after all we have done this term. I am gradually adjusting. I am taking flute lessons again with my old teacher, which gives me a lot of satisfaction, and I am reading all the books I should have read during term but didn't. I am worried about Max. He writes that he is still having terrible doubts about his faith. I don't understand what has precipitated this. He seemed so happy when we parted at the end of term. Luckily he is coming to visit us in a few days so I hope to find out more then. I do hope you are having a good vacation. Have you heard from Adam?

Much love, Hannah

Lucy was touched and embarrassed by this last. Lucy still had no idea that her love for Adam was clear for all to see. To her it was still a secret. As for Max, he seemed the last person to have doubts; he was so solid and straightforward. But then she remembered the conversation they had had at the dinner party about self-doubt. Max had said he doubted himself all the time, and Jeremy had scoffed at him. And surely faith was the most difficult thing to hold on to.

She wrote back,

Dear Hannah,

Very glad to get your letter. I do hope you and Max can have a good talk. I have always thought that faith is what keeps you going when you don't have any faith and don't know where to get any. So perhaps Max will find his again soon if he just endures this time of "aridity." So glad about the flute lessons. Adam has just sent me a postcard in which he describes eating Topfenknodeln at a wonderful restaurant in Vienna. (They are the most delicious little cheese dumplings.)

Love, Lucy

Sarah wrote,

Dear Lucy,

God, Christmas was so boring. We had the turkey and the Christmas pudding like every other single family. Just a lot of cooking and washing up. But I've seen my friend Claire again, who is now at London University, and we've had some wonderful talks. She's very involved with the Labour Party and has inspired me to join in Cambridge. It would be a new direction for me.

My father and I go for long walks on the moors, they are heavenly. Otherwise I am reading and reading. I hope you are enjoying yourself. Have you heard from Adam?

Sarah

Lucy ignored the last question and wrote back,

Dear Sarah,

Wonderful to hear from you and that you are enjoying yourself. I think my parents particularly would be very happy to hear you are joining the Labour party. They think I am lacking in political involvement. I am working at a secondhand bookshop and quite enjoying it; that's my contribution to society.

Love, Lucy

Lucy finally wrote to Adam, but in deference to Anthea, she wrote a postcard, not a letter:

Dear Adam,

Wonderful to receive your card. The Topfenknodeln sound delicious. I am enjoying being at home and going for walks in Greenwich Park every day. Saw Macbeth at the Old Vic. I love Lady Macbeth; she is such a wonderful criminal! Looking forward so much to your return.

Very much love from Lucy

The final greeting had been thought about for a long time.

Then Jeremy telephoned, as Lucy had feared he would. When he invited her to the cinema she asked him to come over for Sunday lunch instead. It was safer, she thought—less intimate, fewer opportunities for Jeremy to fumble for her hand in the dark. Her family would be there, and they could all go for a walk after lunch. He agreed, slightly reluctantly.

On Sunday Jeremy arrived promptly, carrying a bunch of flowers for Mrs. Page. He was wearing a brown tweed jacket and a red bow tie, and looked, as usual, very cheerful. Lucy's father offered him a glass of Cinzano as a change from sherry, and they all sat in the living room together.

"What are you reading?" asked Mr. Page, his inevitable opening gambit that he used with her friends.

"Chemistry," said Jeremy, "but I love all kinds of science."

"Then you'll have to come with us after lunch and see the Greenwich museum with John Harrison's wonderful clocks," said Mr. Page.

"Oh yes," said Lucy, "They are really amazing. They were designed to keep accurate time at sea so that sailors could calculate their longitude, and they worked. But Harrison never really got credit for them."

"The rule of life," said Jeremy laughing.

"What do you mean?" asked Mrs. Page.

"Oh, just that so often good people don't get rewarded for what they've done, and bad people get rewarded unfairly," replied Jeremy.

"That's so cynical," said Anthea. "Do you really believe life is so unfair?"

"Yes I do," said Jeremy, "But that doesn't mean you can't enjoy it. You just have to lower your expectations about being rewarded for doing the right thing."

"But do you still believe in doing the right thing?" asked Lucy, suddenly worried about Jeremy's morals.

"Yes, of course," said Jeremy, "but it's very hard to know what's right and to do what's right if there is a cost to doing it."

"Enough questions for Jeremy," said Mrs. Page. "Come into the dining room for lunch."

Lunch was roast lamb, roast potatoes, and cauliflower with a cheese sauce—Lucy's favorite meal. Her father carved the lamb at the table and everyone tucked in.

Anthea said, "I've joined the Labour Party in Oxford and I'm meeting so many interesting people."

"Yes, that's wonderful, Anthea," said her father. Her mother beamed as she was bringing in the apple crumble. "You'll keep the Tories on their toes!" she said.

"Oh," said Jeremy, "But I am a Tory—at least I voted conservative in the last election—so I suppose that makes me one."

There was an awkward silence. Anthea finally said, "But what about South Africa—you don't support the government there, do you?"

"No, I don't think I do," said Jeremy.

"That's a bit halfhearted," said Anthea. "Surely you don't think apartheid is a just system?"

"No, of course not," replied Jeremy, "it's just a question of how you avoid a bloodbath there."

Jeremy and Anthea talked back and forth in a friendly way, and Lucy thought he did seem to get on well with her family. After lunch, Jeremy, Mr. Page, and Lucy went for a walk in the park and then to the museum to see Harrison's clocks. Jeremy was suitably impressed. They walked down the steep hill to the Cutty Sark—the last clipper ship—in all its splendor, and went into the Naval Museum to look at the relics of Nelson. Lucy was ghoulishly fond of the bloody shirt with the hole in it made by the bullet that had killed Nelson. It made the history seem so recent.

Jeremy and Mr. Page seemed to get on well, in spite of Jeremy's political confession. Jeremy asked Mr. Page about the state of the economy, and Mr. Page explained it at some length. He spoke only to Jeremy, seeming to have quite forgotten that economics was Lucy's subject and that she might have views too. They returned to the house for tea, and Jeremy left soon afterwards. Lucy walked him back to the train through the park. Jeremy said, "I've had such a super time with you and your family. I'm glad I came. It's so nice to see you with your mother. She's lovely." He sighed. As the train came Jeremy hugged Lucy good-bye. "You've been wonderful," he said. "Thank you for such a lovely day. We'll see each other in Cambridge."

Lucy waved good-bye with a full heart. She found herself caring about Jeremy despite herself.

When she got home her father greeted her with, "What a nice young man; he's the salt of the earth. Now why couldn't you fall for someone like him instead of a foreigner from a landlocked country with no naval tradition?" So Lucy knew that her mother had told him about Adam. She didn't care; Cambridge was only a week away, and she was now longing to return to her own room in Oldwick and her new life there.

14

The Earthquake

Christmas vacation was over and it was the beginning of Lent term. Lucy's spirits lifted. She was back in the most beautiful town, the weather was springlike, and the aconites and snowdrops were beginning to bloom. Most importantly, she could now see Adam again. From the moment she set foot in Cambridge she wanted to run over to his room to see if he was back. She couldn't wait to tell him about her Christmas and to hear all about Vienna. Maybe she could take Anthea's advice and ask him about their relationship, where it was going, what lay in store for them. She wanted him to kiss her so that she could feel that melting bliss they had found in Botolph's Lane. However, in spite of all her longings and in spite of Anthea, she decided to wait until he let her know that he wanted to see her. On her first day back, she heard nothing from him. But she thought it was just too early. He must be busy getting unpacked, seeing his supervisor, and so on. It was a consolation to be back among her Oldwick friends, who fell on each other with delight when they all met at dinner. Certainly she faced a great deal of work, and she was determined to do well. At the same time, she had been accepted into the orchestra and would sing in the Oldwick choir, not to speak of all the parties and outings that would take place outside when the weather eventually became warmer. The days were full, but she still woke up every morning thinking of Adam. That had become a way of life to her, part of her daily experience.

On the next day, there was still no word or call. She went for a long walk with Hannah to ease her anxiety. She listened to Hannah's worries about Max as closely as she could and made sympathetic noises. But all her thoughts were of the day she and Adam had spent at Ely, of her profound religious experience in the cathedral, and her love for him in that sacred space. Surely he couldn't forget the deep connection they had made then.

At last, on the fourth day back, she received a note from Adam saying that he would be very glad if she would come to his rooms on Wednesday at eight o'clock for a drink. Lucy was thrilled, but also mystified. There was an air of formality about the note that she did not understand. Perhaps he had decided that he wanted to renew their relationship. Perhaps he would kiss her again. She rushed next door to tell Sarah the news, complaining "But what shall I wear? He's seen my one dress?" Sarah was unimpressed. She had never said so, but Lucy thought she did not like Adam and disapproved of their friendship. However, Sarah generously said, "You can look at my dresses if you like. There's a nice brown one which I never wear, but it might suit you." It was perfect. The dress was of brown wool, a fitted sheath with a short skirt that showed off Lucy's legs—her best physical asset, she had always thought. She took it back to her room and began thinking about which of her three chains to wear with it.

Wednesday came. At five o'clock Lucy was in her room contemplating the evening with pleasure when the door was flung open and Fiona stood there, looking absolutely radiant in her black silk, low-cut dress adorned with what looked suspiciously like a diamond necklace. "I'm just off to my tutor for a sherry party," she said "but Adam wanted me to give you a message. Could you come at 8:30 instead of 8:00 as he's got a dinner?" Lucy was startled. It wasn't just that she had to wait another half hour before she could see her beloved but that the message was sent via Fiona, whom Adam must have already seen since he got back—and must also have seen her that day. She didn't see what Fiona should have to do with her relationship with Adam. Fiona was completely irrelevant. Lucy was puzzled. Nevertheless, she put on the brown dress and went down to dinner with unusual pleasure in her own appearance. Fiona had disappeared from her mind.

As she cycled over to King's she felt completely happy. Only Adam, she thought, could fill her heart like this. Just the idea of seeing him was life-giving. She looked around and everything seemed more vivid than ever before. As she crossed the river over the Cam and looked downstream along the Backs, the overhanging trees could just be made out as dark masses, lit occasionally by lights from the buildings. She turned left along Kings Parade and arrived at King's, where she locked her bike in the rack and almost ran toward his room.

Adam came to the door as immaculately dressed as always, wearing a smooth blue sweater over his shirt and tie. He looked at her appraisingly, apparently with approval, and said, "Come in and sit down by the fire." The room was nice and warm. "But sit in this chair," said Adam, "not on the floor in the Oldwick way." He guided her to a rather formal upright chair facing the couch upon which he sat without offering her anything; no tea, no drink, nothing. Lucy looked around the room. She had been here only once before. Unlike its state at her last visit, it was impeccably neat, and the desk was virtually clear of papers. Now at last they could rekindle their friendship. In this neat room their passion could grow. She looked at him with love, waiting for him to come to her and kiss her. But he had an odd look on his face and seemed to be very restrained. Instead of a kiss, he asked seriously, "How are you?"

"Oh, I'm fine," said Lucy. "I had a really nice Christmas vacation at home, but I'm very glad to be back in Cambridge. It always looks so beautiful. I know it's trite to say, but the Backs are just so magnificent when you see them from the bridge across the river, and the view of King's is breathtaking." She felt she was babbling but couldn't stop. She couldn't think of anything interesting to add, so she said, "How was your vacation? How was it in Vienna?"

"That's a very nice dress," he said, ignoring her question.

"I borrowed it from Sarah," she confessed. He looked uncomfortable, crossing his legs several times and did not seem to know how to respond. "Oh God," she thought "maybe I shouldn't have said that." There was silence. Lucy was thinking that she wanted to kiss him, now. She wanted to go and sit next to him on the couch and put her arms round him and feel that blissful kiss that made her heart leap. Then Adam said, "I'm going to marry Fiona."

Lucy heard the words and felt herself falling. She almost felt dizzy. The room was a dimly lit cave in which she was trapped. She could neither move nor speak. The silence lengthened. Finally it became too painful to her. She went deep inside and pulled out the words she knew she ought to say. Her voice was low, almost a whisper: "I hope you'll be very happy," she managed to say, looking down at her brown dress. She wanted to cry out, "But you know you love only Gabriele. You know she is your true beloved. Fiona isn't; she's just a convenience." But the words did not come. In that moment of insight Lucy knew that she had never had a chance with Adam. She was not his great beloved at all. But Fiona! Did he really love Fiona?

He seemed surprised, relieved by her response. "Thank you," he said. "We'll be getting married at Easter." Everything was suddenly clear to Lucy: Fiona's radiant appearance, and her delivering the message after seeing Adam that day. They had obviously talked about her and decided that Adam should tell her the news today—to deliver the blow as soon as possible. They both knew it would be a blow. Lucy was deeply humiliated by the idea of this little conspiracy—how to tell the rejected lover of her fate. How could she have failed to see that the relationship between Adam and Fiona was so close? She had simply ignored all the signs. She had been so caught up in her own love that she could not see Fiona's. But what kind of love was that, she wondered. Certainly Fiona was flirtatious and admiring, as if all the men she knew were stars. But she wondered how Adam could like this. Surely he could see it for its artificiality. Surely he could see through the gush. But Lucy could not bear it that Adam should be so reduced in her thoughts when her love for him was so strong and true.

"I think I should go home," she said, her voice still peculiarly low and constricted. She got up off the chair and started to fumble around for her coat. "I'll come with you and walk you home," said Adam. "I'm on my bike," she replied, wanting very much to be alone with her grief. "I'll walk your bike for you," said Adam, and Lucy did not have the strength to resist. As he helped her put on her coat he said, "I do care for you very much." Lucy turned away. There was a chasm between "care for" and "love," and she was falling into it. She did not want to hear him speak to her again. They walked back through the quiet, dark streets of Cambridge. Adam seemed almost cheerful. The bad news had been conveyed; he did not seem to feel the shaking of the earthquake he had just created in Lucy's life. He said good-bye to her as they reached her college and said he would pay her a visit soon. Lucy did not reply. She went to her room and flung herself on the bed. No tears came; she could not cry. She felt the pain of nothingness arise from her inner being and encompass her. She got up and pulled off the brown dress and flung it on a chair. She got into bed again and disappeared.

Lucy spent a fitful, miserable, endless night. She could not sleep, and the pain would not stop. When morning finally came and light was streaming in through her window, she forced herself to get up. Adam was lost to her. He did not love her, he loved Fiona. The thoughts came fast as the door clanged, leaving her in a prison of pain. She did not know how to go on. She had given herself to Adam, and he had taken the gift and thrown it away. She was desolate. She got up and dressed and went next door to Sarah's room to return the brown dress. "Adam is marrying Fiona," she said, and finally started to cry. Great sobs came from her. Sarah was not very sympathetic. "Look," she said "you're well out of it. He's just not a very nice man." This was not what Lucy wanted to hear. Adam was still her beloved. Why couldn't Sarah understand the magnitude of her loss? She continued to cry, and Sarah gave her a mug of tea. "I know now he couldn't choose me," Lucy sobbed, "but how can he love Fiona? She just doesn't deserve him."

"Well evidently, since they're together, they deserve each other," said Sarah. Lucy drank her tea and went back to her room, where she cried for a long time.

The next few days were hell. Lucy could hardly move; it was as if she were walking in treacle. She had to fight to move her arms and legs. Her thoughts were all of Adam, and the pain in her heart was agony. She was in a dark space—no room, no furniture, no trees, nothing. The space was very intense with pain, hot with pain. She didn't exist except to feel the pain. She had no form of heart or mind. She was just pain. There was no world, no place where she was, nothing to orient her in the pain. There was no other person there at all. Of course not; how could there be anyone else? She was paralyzed, not even a human being. She knew this suffering could not change. It was immutable. It was who she was. Saint Teresa was wrong. Suffering did not stretch the soul, it destroyed it.

Lucy struggled through the next few days, dragging herself to lectures and trying to write her essays. On Saturday night she had nothing to do. The rooms of all her friends were empty, and there was no one about. She decided to spend the evening in the college library. She got her books and papers together and was walking along the corridor toward the library when she encountered Adam and Fiona walking toward her, holding hands. They were all dressed up and evidently going out for the evening. As they passed her they said "hello," and Lucy managed a faint smile. Then they were gone.

Lucy was at the library door. She turned round and walked back. She left the college and started walking in the night toward the river, dark and slowly flowing. Lucy stared into it. It looked quite deep. She looked around and saw a disheveled man standing a little way off. She didn't know what he was doing there, but he was looking at her. She continued to look into the river. "If I jumped," she thought, "it would be very cold, and I have my shoes on so I would probably sink." Then she thought, "I know I would try to swim. So what good is it to jump? And then I would be so ashamed if I came back to college all wet and had to confess that I had jumped in the river. And then what would that odd man do if I jumped?" She looked toward the man who was still watching her intently. Slowly and reluctantly she turned away from the river and made her way back to her room.

15

The Socialists

The Lent term was full under way. Lucy was living under a cloud. Adam's engagement to Fiona was now public knowledge, and she at last confided her disappointment to her friends. She bore the humiliation of being publicly rejected, but since she also saw it as her fault, not Adam's, she felt she deserved no sympathy and did not ask for any. She had misinterpreted her whole relationship with Adam, and had been blind to his attraction to Fiona. She had based her whole life on one kiss. She should have known better. So she took gratefully the concern of her friends whom she knew were trying to help her, and concentrated on her studies. She still played in the quartet with Fiona as an act of defiance, not a measure of how little she cared—but did not go out with Max and Hannah together any more. The idea of being with a couple in love was too much for her. She was as friendly to Fiona as she could possibly be, and bore up when Fiona appeared to be extremely nice and sympathetic to her. "Noblesse oblige," Lucy called it to herself.

But Charlotte was enraged on her behalf. "What a bastard!" she said when she heard the news. "How he could choose Fiona over you is incomprehensible." Lucy was shocked by the epithet but gratified by the sentiment. She felt relieved that Charlotte was also in a single state. They began to spend a lot of time with each other, having tea, going to the cinema and, always, talking. When they talked about men, one of Charlotte's favorite topics, Lucy found she had become a cynic. She told herself that she no longer believed in love and often thought she was coming close to Sarah's point of view.

"Perhaps all feminists have been disappointed in love," she said to Charlotte as they sat on the floor together in Charlotte's room.

"But that's not true of Sarah; she's never been in love," replied Charlotte.

"True, but maybe she's the exception."

"Well, I'm still looking for a man," said Charlotte, "and I expect to find one before I leave Cambridge."

"I don't know what I want," said Lucy softly. But she did; she still wanted Adam. No matter how hard she tried she could not stop loving him.

One day Hannah came to her room. "I want to talk about Max," she said. Lucy did not feel like having such a conversation given her state of mind about love, but she welcomed Hannah, who had always been a good friend to her, and said, "Why? What's wrong?" Hannah said, "When Max visited me at home in Manchester, he was very downcast and said he just couldn't find God any more. He said he had been a strong believer since before he could remember; that he always thought he had a religious gene, but now everything seemed false to him and he felt disoriented."

"So what did you say to him?"

"Well, at first I was sympathetic," said Hannah, "and I gave him *Interior Castle* to read following your letter and your idea about that you must have faith that you will find your faith again. 'This is just a stop on the road to finding God,' I said; 'St. Teresa has described exactly what you are going through.' And then he asked me what I thought. So I said that I never demanded of God what he seemed to want—a direct connection. For me God is an idea that I find wonderful. I love what Jesus says and am prepared to try to live my life in his footsteps. But I don't worry about whether God answers my prayers. I don't think of God as an omnipotent being at all. Rather, he's the source of love to me. You can't demand that God's grace will fall upon you; you can only wait and hope that you recognize it when it comes. So Jesus says that you have to keep your lamp burning in case he comes." Hannah stopped and looked at Lucy. "I just told him all that and he wasn't comforted at all. Instead he said, 'If I just have you, I should be content, but somehow it's not enough. I need God, and he is gone from me.'"

Then Hannah started to cry. "I just don't understand him, he mystifies me. How can he actually tell me that I am not enough for him? It all makes me feel so inadequate as if there's something wrong with me."

"Of course it's not you," said Lucy, moved by Hannah's tears. "I suppose it's just something he has to go through by himself."

"But that's what's so difficult about it," said Hannah blowing her nose." He's not doing it by himself. He will keep talking to me about it. He tells me he's read everything he can about how people have found their faith and how they held on to it through difficult times and that still doesn't help. I feel so helpless and sometimes so angry. He just won't take comfort from me. I mean, we still spend all our spare time together and study and play music, and sometimes we kiss, but it just doesn't seem the same."

Lucy felt very sympathetic toward Hannah. It did seem like an intractable problem, and she knew what it felt like to be shut out.

"But Hannah, you just said that you can't demand God's grace and that the only thing you can do is wait and see what happens," she said. "Maybe

Max will soon find the light he seeks, and, if he does, it will surely be because of your love for him."

"Oh, Lucy, you always know what to say," said Hannah. "You're such a comfort." She got up and suddenly gave Lucy a quick hug before she left.

Sarah was the next visitor. She came round that evening after dinner and sat on the bed and talked about her new life. Lucy was beginning to feel like a counselor, but she did not dislike the role. Her disappointment had made her much more sympathetic to others and willing to listen. Sarah's Circle had collapsed. Anne refused to come, Hannah was too busy and seemed no longer interested, and Lucy and Charlotte felt they had heard all the lessons that Sarah had attempted to teach them.

Lucy thought that Sarah had come to talk about all this, but in fact Sarah had other news to report. She was now totally involved with Labour Party activities at both the local and national levels. She had found a new set of socialist friends and declared that she was extremely happy. She went every Friday night to the meetings of the University Socialist Club where students met to discuss the philosophy and economics of socialism. On Mondays she went to the meeting of the local Labour Party ward which consisted of eight older women, one old gentleman, and Sarah. She told Lucy that she found the Monday meeting just as interesting as the socialist club, and described it.

The ward meeting was run by a very fat Mrs. Gibbs, who was a stickler for protocol. The secretary, a slightly younger Mrs. Walsh, would be called on to read the minutes of the last meeting, which were then amended and approved by a show of hands. The new business was usually to discuss aspects of national Labour Party policy, but at election time they had to discuss choosing a candidate and the whole business of canvassing. There was always a raffle, the prize consisting of a jar of jam or a box of biscuits. All the discussion had to be directed at the chair, Mrs. Gibbs, and there were to be no side discussions at all. Sarah said. "Lucy, do come to the next meeting with me; I need your moral support. I've got to talk about inflation. I know you've already helped me so much with understanding the economics of it, but I really would like you to be there in case I start getting into a muddle." Lucy said she'd love to go and was really looking forward to meeting the various characters whom Sarah had described.

The community center hall in which the meeting was held was very large, cold, and almost empty. At the far end, two rows of chairs had been set up to face each other. In front of these rows was a table behind which sat the rotund Mrs. Gibbs and the secretary, Mrs. Walsh. They greeted Sarah warmly and acknowledged Lucy. Sarah and Lucy then sat in the lefthand row near the front table, as Sarah was going to be asked to speak. The old gentleman shuffled in with some of the other women, all middle-aged and looking somehow very much alike with their dark coats and scarves, graying hair, and worn faces.

Everyone nodded to each other and sat down. Just before the meeting was due to start, Lucy noticed that a new person had arrived and was sitting at the back end of the rows on the right, opposite her and Sarah. He was a young man with long, reddish-brown hair that fell to his shoulders. He had a handsome face and was wearing blue jeans and a red patterned sweater. He had boots on his feet and looked like an American cowboy. Everyone stared, and Mrs. Gibbs simply acknowledged him by smiling and nodding in his direction.

The main topic for discussion this evening was inflation and unemployment. Following Lucy's guidance, Sarah spoke about the difference between cost-push and demand-pull inflation. "In cost-push inflation," she explained, "prices rise because workers are demanding higher wages and firms raise their prices to cover these extra costs. But in demand-pull inflation, prices rise because there is so much demand from consumers for goods and services that prices go up to ration the excess demand. The difficulty for policymakers is how to tell the difference between the two when all you observe is prices rising." Lucy nudged Sarah as she sat down and whispered, "Well done, that was exactly right." Sarah smiled.

"That was very clarifying, Miss Hardy," said Mrs. Gibbs approvingly. "Does anyone have any questions?"

"I do," said the man at the back. Everyone turned their heads to look at him.

"May I have your name?" asked Mrs. Gibbs.

"Yes, ma'am, it's Tom, Tom Farley," he said in an American accent. Mrs. Gibbs beamed. The only woman in England who was ever called Ma'am was the Queen.

"What is it you would like to say, Mr. Farley?" she asked.

"I'd like to ask Miss Hardy if she thinks that incomes policy is the solution to cost-push inflation. Does she agree that we have to persuade the unions to keep a lid on wage increases to stop prices from rising too fast?"

Sarah was flummoxed. Lucy had told her about incomes policy but Sarah had not fully understood it. But she was determined to hold her own, so she said, "I think we have to be really careful before we ask workers to give up wage increases. Who is going to stop firms from raising their prices anyway and reaping extra profits?"

At a sign from Mrs. Gibbs, Tom replied, "Then I guess Miss Hardy always supports the unions' demands, no matter what."

This was not exactly what Sarah meant, but she thought it best to bow out of the discussion at this point. It was taken up by Mrs. Walsh and the old gentleman, Mr. Simpson, Mrs. Walsh arguing that it was time for the unions to be brought under control and Mr. Simpson saying that Mrs. Walsh and others who supported an incomes policy were betraying the whole meaning of socialism and worker power.

After the collection for the raffle, Mrs. Gibbs brought the meeting to a close and everyone moved to the back of the room, where a table was set up for tea and biscuits. Tom moved to Sarah's side. "I do love English tea so much," he said. "It's as strong as the coffee we drink in the States." He took a cup and sipped it noisily.

"I love it too," said Sarah. "Even children here are given tea; at home we called it milky tea."

"England is a fine place," said Tom, "and especially Cambridge. Are you both students?" Here he nodded to include Lucy.

"Oh yes, we're at Oldwick," replied Sarah, "what about you?"

"Oh, I'm a graduate student in history," he said. "I'm doing research on the labor movement in England in the nineteenth century. I've come from Harvard, but I grew up in the South—Atlanta. I was very impressed by your knowledge of economics. Are you an economics student?"

"Oh no, no," said Sarah hastily, "the economist is Lucy. I'm reading English, focused on nineteenth-century women's literature. But I'm also very interested in women's issues, and I think they fit in with socialist thinking."

Lucy saw Tom looking at Sarah with apparently growing interest. "I know we've just had tea," he said, "But would you both like to come to a pub with me and have a glass of beer?"

Half an hour later they were ensconced in the Black Dog, sitting at the bar this time, and talking about everything together. Sarah was unusually animated. It seemed to Lucy as if she had lost a bit of her hardness. Sarah seemed amazed that a man would actually like to talk about the problems of women, and Tom didn't even balk at her frequent references to the patriarchy; he just smiled politely and sipped his beer. Sarah evidently liked his opinions and his old clothes; he was bohemian, and he supported civil rights for everyone. He asked Sarah if she had read any Edith Wharton, and when she said no, he offered to find her one of her books and bring it to her. Lucy felt she was in the way and soon got up to leave. She thanked Tom very much for the beer, to which he replied "You're welcome," a new expression for her. Sarah waved vaguely in her direction as she left. She had no doubt Sarah would tell her later how the rest of the encounter went.

About an hour later, Sarah came to Lucy's room. Lucy was expecting her and had made two cups of cocoa. Sarah said at once, "So what did you think of the meeting?"

"Well, I think you were brilliant," replied Lucy warmly. "You were so poised and self-possessed, I really admire you. And I found the meeting very interesting, though I did wonder how a tiny ward meeting like that could have an influence on Labour Party policy. But we must get the Tories out, and I suppose that's the place to start."

"But what did you think of Tom?" asked Sarah, completely ignoring what Lucy had just said.

"Well, I think he liked you a lot," said Lucy.

"Oh, do you think so?" asked Sarah, sipping her cocoa. "I found him very interesting."

"So then I suppose you don't consider him as part of the patriarchy?" asked Lucy innocently.

Sarah actually blushed. "Well he is a man, so he's clearly benefited from it. How many women go from Georgia to Harvard? But I must say he seemed to be very interested in rights for women."

"Well, that's all right then," said Lucy, who was enjoying Sarah's struggle to come to terms with the idea that she liked Tom.

LLL

A week later, Sarah came back to Lucy to describe the meeting of the student socialist society she had been to, which Tom had also attended. Tom had sat next to her, she told Lucy with a gratified smile. He asked her who the speaker was for the evening. She told him it was a Professor Levine, who was going to talk about how centrally planned economies like the Soviet Union work. Professor Levine was an excellent speaker, wonderfully clear and very knowledgeable about his field. Sarah told Lucy she was quite uplifted to hear the lecture with Tom. It was evident that Tom did not enrage her as other men did. He was so low key and unconventional.

They had gone out together afterward with a group from the society. Everyone was very interested in Tom, and he responded warmly to requests to describe his country and his philosophy. He rejected various challenges that he was a capitalist in disguise, or worse still, a CIA agent. He certainly did not look like one, and had no notebook. At the end of the evening he had walked Sarah home to Oldwick and asked her out for the next Saturday night—for a date, he called it.

"Isn't that wonderful?" asked Sarah, looking at Lucy with an almost pleading look on her face. Lucy replied dutifully that it was. She was still amazed that Sarah managed to like Tom in spite of his sex and was almost envious that Sarah had a real commitment to a cause whereas she had nothing. It seemed to Lucy that all her friends were happy and involved and that she was left on the sidelines, wallowing in her grief.

Adam had visited her a week after "that night" as she referred to it in her mind. He had been cheerful and friendly and apparently oblivious to the pain he had caused her. "How are you?" he had asked, "and what are you doing these days?"

"I'm fine," Lucy had said, feeling that it was her turn to be cool and detached. "I'm just finishing an essay and then I have to practice my cello part for the orchestra. Did I tell you that I was asked to join this term? We're playing Beethoven's Fifth, and there are lots of tricky cello passages." She had been both deeply happy to see him and at the same time full of pain. She saw him at once as a traitor and a beloved object of her passion. She felt that he had deceived her, but at the same time that she had no right to his love. But she knew that if he were to break with Fiona she would be there, waiting once more for him. She said, "Why have you come to see me?"

Adam looked surprised, and said simply "I've come because I hope we can be friends."

Lucy couldn't bear to be his friend when she wanted to be his lover. Did he really think that she should somehow suppress all her longings and behave to him like a sister? But she had said, "Oh, yes, of course, we already are."

"I'm so pleased," said Adam. "I was hoping that you would say that. And Fiona will be pleased too."

"That's a stretch," thought Lucy unkindly, but she caught herself when she remembered how nice Fiona had been to her in the quartet lately. Maybe they truly wanted her friendship. She replied, "Oh yes, Fiona and I have been getting on so well in the quartet; we have great fun."

Adam looked around the room in a vaguely interested manner. "Oh," he said, "I see you have a copy of the book about Klimt's *Beethoven Frieze*."

"Yes," said Lucy, "Jeremy gave it to me."

"Ah," said Adam. "Have you seen the real thing in Vienna?"

"Yes," she said.

Adam looked at her expectantly, but she said nothing more. He got up to leave. "I hope I can visit you again soon," he said. Lucy had such mixed feelings about this that she could barely say, "That would be nice."

After this visit by Adam Lucy was cast down and sick of her Englishness. Deep inside she felt furious, but she could not bring herself to shout and slam doors as she had done as a child. All she had to fall back on was her good manners. The idea that she and Adam could be friends was absurd, but she went along with Adam's wishes. Only the familiar pain welled up in her heart, and she cried yet again for her lost passion.

A few days later she was cheerfully surprised when Jeremy looked round her door and said, "Any Cinzano going?" Lucy laughed and said, "You're in luck. My father gave me a bottle to bring back with me, and here it is." She poured them both a glass. "How are you, Jeremy?" she asked.

"Jolly well," he said, "the chemistry is really becoming exciting and I've been doing a lot of photography. Would you let me do a portrait of you?"

"Good heavens," cried Lucy, "whatever for?"

"Don't be so surprised," he said, "the photography club is having a competition, and I want to enter my picture of you – that is if it comes out as well as I think it will."

"But why on earth would you ask me?" said Lucy.

"Because you have a phenomenal face, very mobile and expressive," he replied.

"Don't be silly, my face is perfectly ordinary. Why don't you ask Fiona? Now there's a pretty face!"

"No," said Jeremy firmly, "It's got to be your face, I'll have no other."

"Well, all right, if you must," said Lucy capitulating. "Where do you want to do it?"

"The club has a studio with lots of equipment. If you could come there that would be great." In spite of herself, Lucy was pleased by this invitation. She was glad that Jeremy liked her face, and the compliment went a long way toward relieving her low spirits.

The photo session took place a few days later. Jeremy told her to put her hair up in a chignon, and then later they could try some shots with it falling around her shoulders. She was very excited as she arrived at the studio on the second floor of a house on Tennison Road. Jeremy was there with Anne. Lucy had hardly seen her this term, and she greeted her warmly. "Anne is here to help me," said Jeremy. "She's very good with poses." Anne seemed pleased to see her, but Lucy felt guilty. Surely Jeremy should be taking Anne's photograph, not hers. She had seen how happy Anne had been with Jeremy at the playing party, and now Jeremy was paying her all this attention and asking Anne to help. She really did not want to be part of another triangle.

"Now sit on this stool," said Jeremy, "and let your face go in repose. Not smiling yet. Turn slightly away from me. Well done, that's perfect." He took several shots and then remarked, "Your expression is so sad, Lucy, I think we need to lighten it up a bit. So think of something jolly in your life," he said. Lucy could not think of anything jolly at all, her life was all grief. But Jeremy stood in front of her waving and telling jokes and she laughed in spite of herself. She felt like a film star, with Jeremy and Anne moving her around in various ways, telling her to look up, look down. Then Jeremy said, "Now let your hair down and we'll do some shots like that." She did as she was told, and it felt like disrobing in public. Anne combed her hair for her and said, "Now that's perfect, you have such pretty hair." Jeremy snapped away, and Lucy felt lifted up and happy. She had never received such concentrated attention since the days of Mrs. Clark and Professor Pracht, and she loved it. Jeremy said "Jolly good, excellent, now that's a good one" after every shot, and she felt like a beautiful person.

She was thrilled when she finally saw the photos. One showed her laughing, with her hand up to push her hair out of her face. It had never occurred to her that she could look either interesting or glamorous, and she was diffident when she asked Jeremy for some copies so that she could show her parents. The photo that Jeremy and Anne entered into the competition did not win, but Jeremy did not seem too disappointed. He took to visiting Lucy quite frequently, and Lucy found herself buying more Cinzano to offer him. She now looked on him as a dear friend in spite of his pimples and greasy hair. She did not once think that she was leading him on in any way, nor did she think much more about the effect their friendship was having on Anne. She had no romantic thoughts about Jeremy at all and couldn't imagine that he had any about her.

Adam was also a regular visitor. These visits she tolerated and never questioned. She took him at his word that he wanted to be friends with her and never had the courage to tell him not to come any more. One day toward the end of term he entered her room with a purposeful manner. "I want to talk to you," he said, "and look, I've brought you a present."

Wordlessly, Lucy took the gift. "Open it," he said. Inside was a beautiful jade necklace. "Fiona and I thought this would just suit you," he said.

Lucy felt overwhelmed. At last she found her voice. "Thank you both so much," she said formally, "it's really beautiful."

Adam sat down on a chair, took out a cigarette, and lit it. Lucy sat opposite him and wondered what on earth was coming.

"Fiona and I really want you to come to our wedding," he said. "For myself, I really wouldn't feel it was complete if you weren't there, and Fiona considers you a true friend."

All she could think of was that she wanted to give him everything he asked for. He seemed so sincere and genuine.

"We want to be connected to you," he said. "We don't want to lose your friendship after we are married."

All Lucy's cynicism flew out of the window. She loved him and she believed him. He must care for her, even if he didn't love her, and that was now enough for her. She would accept the crumbs from his plate, especially in the form of a necklace.

"All right," she said, "I will be honored to come to the wedding." She did not think that she was letting herself down by accepting his invitation. She thought of it as a wedding gift for Adam that she should be there.

Adam stayed on a while talking about the wedding plans and where he and Fiona planned to go for their honeymoon. When he finally got up to leave, he hugged Lucy and said, "It's so wonderful that you will come. Fiona and I hope that you will visit us after we are married." He kissed her warmly on the cheek and left.

Lucy felt ambivalent about going to the wedding and seeing the gorgeous Fiona dressed up and radiant with happiness. The alternative was to stay at home with no distraction from her familiar state of depression. She had allowed herself to be persuaded to be a friend when she wanted to be a lover. And Fiona's role in all this was not clear. It was hard to believe that she really wanted Lucy at the wedding, especially when it was known by all that Lucy was in love with Adam. Maybe Fiona was vaccinating Adam against her by pretending to be friendly as well. In the end she thought, "I'll go to the wedding and see the bloody deed done, and then I'll know that I can never have him." Such was the reasoning of the lovelorn Lucy.

Part III

Easter Vacation and Easter Term

16

The Wedding

Lent term ended and, once again, Lucy was at home with her family. She was planning to spend two weeks of the Easter vacation in France with Charlotte. But first, there was Adam and Fiona's wedding to be endured. She was still determined to go. Anthea said, "You're a masochist," and Lucy agreed.

The wedding was held in a beautiful flower-filled Catholic church in London. Fiona had recently converted to Catholicism. Lucy knew this was important to Adam but, with her strong Protestant roots, she told herself that she would never have become a Catholic to please anyone, even Adam. However, she supposed, for Fiona who had no strong beliefs, conversion was a social convention that made the whole thing easier, especially where bringing up children was concerned.

For the wedding, Lucy had bought a flowered jacket which she wore with a tight, black skirt and a large red hat. She sat in the back of the church on the groom's side, and she could not see much. She felt strange having come alone. Everyone else who entered was either a couple or with friends. She knew only Adam and Fiona and those two friends of Fiona, Jane and Camilla, but they didn't notice her as they came in all decked out with flowery hats and sat on the other side of the church.

The bride entered on her father's arm wearing an exquisite low-cut, off-the-shoulder white silk dress. She was fully veiled, which seemed to Lucy a contradiction of the daring dress. The ceremony began, a beautiful singer sang, the vows were said, and there was a lot of walking back and forth in front of the altar that Lucy did not understand. She sat through the entire wedding mass, and when the bride and groom disappeared to sign the register she left the church. Tears were coursing down her face. She scrubbed them away and decided that she would go to the reception anyway—she would see this thing through to the end.

Lucy walked over to the restaurant where the reception was being held and found a waiter, who poured her a glass of champagne. Meandering to the window, she looked out on London. Here were people going about their lives, doing good works, being purposeful and happy. What on earth was she doing here, she wondered, when all it gave her was pain? She took a big sip of champagne and vowed that from now on her life would change. There would be no more hopeless love, no more longing, just useful work like the three sisters in Chekhov's play. Work was something you could control and afterward have something to show for it. What, after all, had she achieved by falling in love with Adam? Nothing, nothing at all!

Eventually the wedding party and the guests began to arrive. The guests formed themselves into a loose line to be greeted by the wedding party. But at first the bride and groom were not in the receiving company. Probably yet more photos were being taken. So when Lucy got to the front she was greeted by the bride's parents, the groom's mother and father, and his brother, Peter, without having to face Adam and Fiona. Then she sauntered off, and when she looked again she saw that they had now joined the receiving line. Feeling that she must go through the formalities with them too, she went back through the line, kissed Fiona, shook hands with Adam, and was confronted by Peter again, who looked at her and laughed and said, "Are you teasing us?"

Lucy looked at him as if for the first time. He was not a bit like Adam. He had a ruddy face, light brown hair, and bright, lively blue eyes. His mouth was wide and was, at the moment, laughing at her. She adjusted her hat and laughed back without explaining. She left the line again and joined the other guests who were now drinking the abundant champagne and eating canapés. She was making conversation with them when Peter suddenly appeared beside her, took her arm in a familiar way, and asked her if she needed more champagne. He caught a waiter's eye and exchanged her half-empty glass for a full one, and proceeded to look at her with captivating intimacy.

"What is your name?" he asked. "Are you a Cambridge student too?"

"Oh, I'm Lucy," she replied, "and yes, I'm at Oldwick with Fiona. I play in a quartet with her." As an afterthought she added, "I also know Adam." She blushed when she said this, but Peter's good spirits were so infectious that she began to laugh and talk in a way quite at odds with just having suffered through the final episode of her love for his brother. She was caught up in the warm attentions of Peter, and suddenly the day brightened and the wedding began to seem like a happy affair.

The reception was over, and the bride and groom left for their honeymoon, the bride's mother calling out imperiously, "Come and see her, come and see her, she's leaving now." But for Lucy, the wedding was not yet over. A dinner party had been arranged for the young people in the wedding party at another restaurant where there were to be a band and dancing. Fiona and Adam had included Lucy in this party, a generous gesture that Lucy did not fully appreciate. When she told Peter that she would be joining the wedding party at dinner he looked delighted, and they went together in a taxi to the restaurant. There he seated himself directly opposite her at the table. Lucy was simply swept along.

The music played; more wine and food were served. Lucy found herself telling Peter all about her life, except for the most important thing.

"I loved Vienna," she said, "especially the music. Do you hear the Vienna Philharmonic often? It was so difficult to get tickets that I heard them only twice, but once was the Ninth Symphony, so I can't complain. What do you do there?"

"I'm studying Law," he said, "like everyone else. I have two more years to go, and then I want to go into the Foreign Service." He poured her some more wine, and Lucy was getting decidedly tipsy.

"How exciting," said Lucy. "You must love travel. I think that when you go to another country you become a different person to yourself."

"So how did Vienna change you?" he asked, smiling at her.

"Oh, I suppose I became more independent. When I first left home I had hardly ever gone into a café or restaurant by myself, just Lyons, you know, the cafeteria where you get very strong tea; but in Vienna I was always taking myself out, to cafés mostly. Then, Cambridge is almost like another country – and it is changing me too. You meet so many different people and hear so many different ideas. I even joined a women's circle for a while and learned to despise the patriarchy." She laughed when she said this; she just wanted to talk and talk. Peter seemed really interested despite a sardonic look when she mentioned the patriarchy.

"Tell me about your studies in Law," said Lucy.

"It is very hard work, and each year you have to pass a very difficult exam. I remember in one exam we had a good cheating scheme. The exam questions were surreptitiously dropped out of the window, picked up by the cleverest boy in the next class up, and the answers were smuggled back into the exam by a kind and cooperative maid who came in to empty the rubbish. It was all very risky, but it worked."

Lucy was genuinely shocked. She herself would never have allowed herself to participate in any kind of cheating. But she was unconsciously drawn to cheaters, and she admired them for their ingenuity and courage as well as for their desire to subvert the system. Despite her disapproval she could not think of Peter as a dishonest person; his personality seemed to be so open and forthright. He did not have the controlling, detached air that Adam had. But she did not want to think of Adam now when his wonderful brother was with her. So she laughed at this story and took another big sip of wine.

Peter stood up, walked over to the band, and asked them to play a Viennese waltz. The band obliged with a Strauss waltz, and Peter took Lucy in his arms and waltzed with her around the small dance floor as if they were at a wonderful ball in Vienna. Lucy stumbled a bit at first as she was not used to waltzing at such a quick tempo. She had been to Mrs. Curwin's dancing classes as a teenager, and the boys and girls had shuffled round the room, very shy and awkward as they held each other trying to learn the quickstep and the waltz. The waltz was static and slow, ONE behind, two to the side, three together, ONE behind, two to the side, three together. But in Peter's arms, the waltz went like lightning, and they twirled around, first to the left and then to the right. Lucy was holding on for dear life, her feet moving faster and faster. All the guests in the party clapped their approval.

When they sat down Lucy was breathless and the room was spinning. Some of the other guests had gone, so Peter came and sat next to her and held her hand, which made her tremble.

"I love all music too," he said, "but especially Berlioz. You must listen to his "Symphonie Fantastique"; it is spectacular. Did you go to the opera much? You must come to Vienna to visit me and I will take you to see *Don Giovanni*, the best of all operas. Can you imagine? In the first fifteen minutes there are a rape and a duel, and all sung in the most glorious music you have ever heard."

It was midnight when they left the restaurant. Lucy had missed the last train home and realized she would have to take a taxi. Peter said he would walk her to a taxi rank. They wandered through the London streets and found themselves in Leicester Square. Although it was late it was still full of people coming back from the theater or a restaurant and going into crowded pubs. Clusters of gaily dressed girls spilled out into the street, and groups of laughing men sent catcalls in their direction. The streets were lit up so brightly that it could have been the middle of the day. It had rained, and the neon lights of the cinemas were reflected upward from the damp ground in sparkling colors. Lucy felt the same tingling feeling as when she had seen the Beatles.

She saw a telephone booth and said she should call her mother to let her know that she would be coming home late in a taxi. They both squeezed into the booth and immediately started kissing furiously, completely ignoring the public nature of their situation. Suddenly Lucy caught her breath and held it. Peter's fingers were inside her and were pushing insistently. She hardly knew what was happening. "Is this what they mean when they say a man is fast?" she thought. She had a moment of terror and then continued the kissing with abandon. She didn't know how she made the call or how they ever extricated themselves from the phone booth. She thought, "I love this man." No other word seemed to describe her feelings. This morning she had been miserable and crying at Adam's wedding and now, this evening, she felt deliriously happy with his brother. But she didn't feel confused at all, just tipsy. It all seemed perfectly natural to her. They walked vaguely toward a taxi rank, kissing and nuzzling, and Peter finally put her in a cab and sent her off, saying he would write to her.

She slept fitfully and awoke in an unsettled mood. Peter was going back to Vienna that morning, and she had no idea when she was ever going to see him again or if he would write to her as he promised. She didn't see how they could have a relationship when he was so far away in Vienna, and she felt let down. She told her mother and sister about Peter, but they did not want to hear about another Austrian beau—they had seen Lucy in enough pain from the first. So they ignored Lucy's bad mood, and her mother took her round the streets canvassing for the Labour Party to take her mind off love. Lucy deeply resented this imposed activity, which took her ever further away from the enchanted evening.

Two days later, Lucy received a brief letter from Peter, written on that wedding night and posted in London before he left:

> *Darling Lucy,*
>
> *Thank you for a wonderful evening. I am thinking about you all the time. I want to see you again. When can you come to Vienna? Write to me please.*
>
> *With many kisses and hugs, from Peter*

Thoughts of Adam went completely out of her head. It was as if she had never known him.

17

Vienna Reprise

The Easter vacation had come and gone, and the Easter semester was now half over.

Cambridge was glorious with all the trees and flowers in full bloom. In Emmanuel College the ducks in the duck pond had produced lots of little ducklings that ran around under the old, spreading trees, delighting the students who were reading and sunning themselves on the lawns. In the afternoon and evening the river Cam was full of students lounging in punts while being poled along by one of their number. Everywhere students were working hard for the exams in June.

Life had changed for Lucy. She was happy and industrious. Following Peter's first letter, she had cut short her holiday with Charlotte in Paris and taken the train across Europe to Vienna. She remembered her first journey there, fifteen months before: her wonder at Cologne cathedral, the onion-shaped church towers, and the wonderfully neat farms and villages of Germany and Austria. When she arrived, instead of Frau Mueller, there was Peter waving and smiling at her. He kissed her, put his arm round her, and took her to his tiny VW car. Then they drove to his flat, where she was to stay one week with him. They started kissing as soon as they were inside the door. They immediately fell into bed, and Lucy was initiated into the art of sex.

It was all very surprising – nothing like she had imagined. There was so much physical strenuousness about it, the moving and entwining of limbs, the continuous movement up and down inside her, the mixture of pain and then pleasure, and throughout, the breathing and kissing and murmuring and shouting. Finally they lay exhausted, side by side. Peter said "Ich liebe dich, meine Lucy," and Lucy felt her heart would burst from happiness. It was a startling experience, to be wanted so much by a man and to feel her own desire fulfilled. She felt as if she had crossed the threshold into a new and shining room where the colors and shapes of things were completely different from any she had ever known. She laughed out loud as she thought that this was not what St. Teresa had in mind, and Peter immediately wanted to know what was so funny. She began to explain about *Interior Castle*, but Peter silenced her mid-sentence by kissing her all over again. How extraordinary to feel that her body was really part of her instead of something outside herself that she should be ashamed of. Before, she had always bewailed her body, her small breasts, her unremarkable face; she was too short, and she had nondescript hair. But now she truly felt she was beautiful, and it was a relief from the self-denigration she indulged in when she looked at herself in the mirror. She wondered briefly whether sex before marriage was really as wrong as so many people seemed to think. But this beautiful experience completely contradicted that thought, and she put it out of her mind. As she was dressing afterward she thought about how experienced Peter was. He was loving but also expert. She wondered how he had found such experience and with what woman or women. But the idea of his unknown prior experiences did not distract her from the present reality. He loved her now, and that was all that mattered. She was in no doubt about her own feelings; they had been there from their first meeting.

That afternoon they sat in the Café Mozart near the Opera house, drinking coffee and eating cheesecake as they planned their week. Peter had tickets for *Don Giovanni* that night, and they also bought tickets for the Musikverein, the golden hall where a string quartet was to play. Lucy's memories of her first time in Vienna came flooding back, and she felt the same sense of blissful freedom she had then. But now she was with Peter, and this was a different kind of happiness. This happiness could be shared with him; all her thoughts could be expressed and reflected back to her in Peter's response.

"Do you think men like Don Giovanni really exist?" she asked after they had seen the opera that night. "It's not just that he wants to take all women, but that he's so unrepentant about it. Even when he has to pay the final price of going to hell, he still won't repent."

"I've met lots of men who like to go out with one woman after another," said Peter. "I think they like the feeling of power it gives them, not just the sexual pleasure. I'm not one of those," he added laughing, seeing a curious look on Lucy's face.

"And yet Elvira truly loves him to the end," said Lucy. She began to reflect that she had kept on loving Adam for a long time, but not for ever. She had been saved from her misery by Peter at the wedding. So far neither she nor Peter had mentioned Adam, and she was deathly afraid of the topic. She had no idea what Adam might have told Peter about her and she had no wish to explore the matter, ever. She brushed these thoughts aside; Peter was with her now, with his arm round her in a possessive way, kissing her at odd moments and telling her his thoughts.

"Mozart certainly gives Elvira a lovely aria to express her unrequited love," he said. "I wish the rest of us could sing of our feelings like that. It would be a great consolation."

"Oh," thought Lucy, "so he has suffered too."

The week with Peter was enchanted. As they strolled hand-in-hand through the Volksgarten looking at the rose bushes, she remembered the couple she had watched on that first train ride to Vienna—how they had held hands, and how she had been embarrassed to look, envying them. Now she and Peter were lovers holding hands, and she felt envied by the entire world.

On the third day they went to the Musikverein to hear a string quartet. The program was Haydn, Beethoven, and Shostakovich. Lucy had never really listened to Shostakovich before; his music had always seemed alien to her. But here with Peter she was entranced. The amazingly long, slow phrases played by the strings with impeccably steady bows drew out of her soul all her love and grief. Peter's hand was in hers, and she felt her soul flow into his. It was as if she was now the healer who could sooth any grief, the lover who could bring joy. This powerful feeling that her soul was open and free and that Peter was joined with her in it took her breath away. She sat transfixed as the music ended. When she finally turned toward Peter she saw he was looking at her face and thought she saw tears in his eyes. The applause died away, and they stumbled out of the concert hall clinging to each other as on a shipwreck. That night their lovemaking was quiet and tender. There were no words to be said.

The week flashed by. They talked of everything together. "My father is just like yours seems to be," said Peter. "He's very remote and hard. My mother is lovely; she loves Adam the best. But he and I have always been close friends." Lucy blushed at this mention of Adam and remembered how he had talked to her of his affection for his "little brother." How would Adam react if he knew that she and Peter were lovers? For a moment everything seemed unbearably complicated. Once again she pushed the thought of Adam aside; she didn't want to talk or think about him. She was now a different person from the one who had knelt in Ely Cathedral and felt like a bride.

"My father can't help his sternness," she said. "He behaves like a teacher to us, not a father—always setting high standards. I think fathers should go to school to learn how to relate to their children; it just doesn't seem to come naturally to them."

"I think I could do better," said Peter.

"Of course you could," said Lucy, and the question of children hung in the air between them.

"Dear Lucy," said Peter, "what do you really want?"

Lucy was so taken aback by this question that she fell silent. What she wanted was for Peter to ask her to marry him. He should go on his knees and beg for her hand. But he had turned the question around to her, and she was disappointed. He was asking her to be the first to declare herself, and she was afraid to. She did not want to raise the stakes in their relationship if Peter was not ready. Finally she said, "I just want to be happy with you as we are now. I feel closer to you than I have ever felt with anyone."

Peter seemed satisfied with this answer. He looked at her and smiled. "I think we will never lose touch with each other; we are too close." This was not as strong a statement as Lucy had hoped for, but she was content nonetheless. In his arms she felt that it was just a matter of time until they decided that they would be always for each other and get married.

The next day Peter took Lucy to meet his parents. They lived in a large apartment in a grand old building on the Porzellangasse. Lucy was excited and flattered. She and Peter were invited for afternoon coffee, and as the day was sunny and nice they all sat outside on a veranda overlooking a shady garden. Peter's parents spoke excellent English, like Peter. His father was an old-fashioned Viennese gentleman. He had a stern face and a dry sense of humor. He bent over Lucy's hand very formally when they were introduced and said, "I am delighted to meet the girl from Cambridge." He was impeccably dressed like Adam; his trousers had knife-edge creases in them, and he carefully hitched them up at the knees when he sat down. Lucy was nervous, but Peter was so sunny and at ease with her and his parents that she soon relaxed. A housekeeper brought out the coffee and apricot cake. Peter's mother was lovely, with a generous mouth like Peter's, and bright dark eyes. She poured Lucy's cup and said, "I know in England you drink tea, but here in Austria we love our coffee. Have you enjoyed your time in Vienna?"

"Oh yes," said Lucy, "so very much. I was also here last year for six months and took cello lessons at the Akademie with Professor Pracht." Peter's father seemed impressed by this and said, "The cello is my favorite instrument but it is too late for me to learn now. Neither of the children plays an instrument. It's odd for an Austrian family not to have any real musicians." Peter looked slightly downcast at this statement. His mother hastily said, "But they are all phenomenal skiers." Lucy said, "I once tried skiing but I was very bad at it. All the same I'd love to try it again. The trouble is England doesn't have much snow in the winter, and the mountains are far from London."

The conversation continued in this stilted way and turned to other things – the museums they had seen, the artists they liked. As they left, Peter's father said, "You must come again to Vienna and learn to ski," which Lucy took as an endorsement.

As they were driving home Peter said, "My mother is a true Catholic; she takes her religion very seriously. It's a pity you could not talk to her about that, you would have enjoyed it."

"Are you religious?" asked Lucy.

"Well, I do not have a personal God who speaks to me or to whom I can pray," replied Peter. "But I believe in the teachings of Christianity, in love and forgiveness. I suppose all religions teach that."

"What does that mean—a 'personal God?'" asked Lucy. "Surely the idea of God is that he is accessible to all, that we are all children of God. I don't have a God that speaks only to me either. I just sometimes get the feeling that I am connected to God in love and that love is infinite, like a river flowing through me from an infinite source."

Peter looked at her and appeared moved by her words. He said, "I think God should always be kind to you, Lucy, you are such a beautiful person."

On their last evening together they went to an old-fashioned Viennese restaurant on the Ringstrasse. It had dark wood paneling, tables with radiant white cloths, and racks of newspapers on sticks for easy reading. Peter walked ahead of her into the restaurant in the old style in order to confront the maître d' first. They were seated comfortably at a table by the window. The waiters were very formal and referred to Lucy as "die Dame," which she appreciated. It made her feel indeed like a lady. Peter gave their order to the waiter: the conventional Wienerschnitzel for Lucy, her favorite; goulash for Peter; and then wine. Peter asked her about Cambridge. He wanted to know what it was like and who her friends were.

"That's a lot to tell," laughed Lucy. "It's such a beautiful place, and Oldwick College is very grand, though not as old as the men's colleges. There are still very few women at Cambridge and only four women's colleges. My friend Sarah thinks that's a reflection of the power of the patriarchy to exclude women from full citizenship. I've learned a lot from her, though I don't believe that all men are oppressors, not entirely that is. What do you think about women's lib, I mean liberation?"

"I don't really know what that means," said Peter. "There are many women who study with me at the Uni who also plan to become lawyers, and they are just as competent as the men, often more so. But it becomes difficult for them when they have a family. Most families like that have nannies and other help in the house. But I think a woman herself should take care of the children. Otherwise the nanny becomes the mother and maybe she is not as good a mother as the real one."

Lucy recalled the endless conversations they had had in Sarah's Circle about this point. She became bold. "Why can't fathers take care of the children and mothers go out to work?"

"Oh, that's ridiculous" said Peter. "Only the mother can feed the baby and take care of it. This is not a man's job. Surely that should be clear."

"So do you think women should not work at all?" Lucy persisted.

"It depends on the husband's wishes," replied Peter. "I would not like my wife to work. I think the tasks of men and women should be clearly divided: The woman stays at home and the man goes to work."

"Is that why there are no women in the Vienna Philharmonic orchestra? They're all at home, even gifted violinists?" said Lucy.

"What would women do when the orchestra goes on tour?" responded Peter.

Lucy was not really surprised by Peter's views. She knew from Adam that Austrian men liked to be in control. Also, she really agreed with Peter that women should stay at home to bring up the children, at least when they were young. But there was something in his words that was dogmatic and inflexible, and this was a side of him she had not seen before. She stopped playing devil's advocate and said in a conciliatory voice, "Well, I agree with you about mothers staying at home with the babies."

They looked at each other, laughed, and called a truce.

Dessert came—a wonderful apricot compote. They sipped coffee and talked about how they were going to write to each other often. Lucy said, "You must come to visit me at home in London in the summer. Then we can take a trip to Cambridge and I can show you how lovely it is."

"I would like that very much," said Peter.

The week was over and they had to say good-bye. Lucy cried at the Westbahnhof as they kissed for the last time, and Peter laughed a little at her and said, "It is not so bad, dear Lucy, we will see each other again soon." On the train she found that she couldn't stop crying. She tried to hide it as the compartment was full, but the tears would keep rolling down her cheeks. If only someone would inquire about her and comfort her. But no one did; they all pretended not to notice. Her grief was strange to her. She had had a wonderful week and felt a love and closeness with Peter she had never felt before. She had grown up and become a woman. She should be burning with happiness, but instead she was crying as if she had just broken up with him. She realized that she was afraid of the future. As the train rolled on through Europe toward the Channel coast, the cloud gradually passed, her tears ceased, and her happiness returned. As she had left Peter had said to her, "Everything is open to us; the future will be what we want," and she believed him, felt comforted, and had hope in her heart.

Now she was back in Cambridge for the summer term and looked forward every week to a letter from Austria. When it came, she drank it up. But she did not pine; she had regained her confidence and lived her happiness. She knew they were in love with each other and that she wanted to marry Peter, but she did not mind waiting. She understood that Peter might not want to commit himself so soon and that they needed to get to know each other better. So she took up her work and her friends again and began to enjoy Cambridge in the summer.

One day, Lucy, Jeremy and Anne were sitting in Lucy's room talking. Lucy's friendship with both had grown since the photo shoot, and they were often together as a threesome. Sarah unexpectedly appeared at the door with Tom Farley in tow. "I want you all to meet Tom," she said. She sounded quite matter of fact, but Lucy detected a certain energy that had not been there before. Also, she was dressed differently. She was in fact wearing the famous brown dress that Lucy had worn to Adam's the night of her "funeral," as she referred in her mind to that dreadful evening. The dress showed off Sarah's slim figure. She wore no scarf on her head, and her hair was washed and combed. She looked very pretty.

"Hi, Lucy," said Tom, in a laconic drawl. "Very nice to meet you again."

"Tom's from America," said Sarah to Jeremy and Ann in unnecessary explanation.

"Do come in and sit down," said Lucy. "We can all squash in together; this is Jeremy and this is Anne."

"Hello," said Anne, avoiding Sarah's gaze.

"Hi there!" said Jeremy in an American accent.

"Would you like some sherry?" Lucy asked Tom.

"I'd rather have a beer," he said.

"Oh dear," said Lucy, "I never have beer in my room. The only other thing I have is Cinzano."

"Well, I don't know what that is, but I'll try it," he said. "It will be a change from sherry. I reckon I've drunk more sherry in Cambridge than beer at home."

Lucy laughed and poured them both a glass.

"We wondered if you'd all like to come with us to a talk about South Africa tonight. There's an excellent speaker, and we really should support the fight against apartheid," said Sarah. "The British and American governments still support the South African government and send them arms to be used against black people. It's got to be stopped."

"When did you get so interested in South Africa?" asked Lucy.

"It's a recent thing," said Sarah. "Tom had been telling me about the civil rights struggle of black people in America, and then we both got interested in apartheid. You know we met at that Labour Party ward meeting."

"I guess I'm a socialist of sorts," said Tom, "and I thought I'd find out what was going on in England. So I went to one of the meetings."

"So what brought you to Cambridge?" asked Jeremy.

"Oh, I'm a graduate student in History," he said. "I'm doing research on the nineteenth-century labour movement in England."

"So does that include women's rights?" Jeremy asked with an ironic look at Sarah.

"Oh yes, I'm interested in all forms of social justice, though of course Sarah is the expert on women," he said with a smile that lit up his whole face. Sarah looked pleased as she looked over at Tom; she seemed to have lost her hard edge.

"So where do you stand on the patriarchy?" asked Jeremy.

Tom laughed. "Well, I was brought up in the Deep South, and in our house my mother was queen, so I suppose all I know is a matriarchy."

"Oh, so men don't rule the world in America?" Jeremy persisted.

"Well, I think white men certainly do," said Tom. "And they still do in South Africa, so that's why we want you to come to the talk."

Tom was so gracious and witty as Jeremy put him on the spot that Lucy could see exactly why Sarah liked him. He and Sarah exchanged glances frequently and smiled at one another, as if they were a couple. Lucy could hardly believe it.

"I'll come; what about you both?" said Lucy, looking at Anne and Jeremy.

"Count me out," said Jeremy. "I've got a ton of work to do tonight."

"I'll come if you're going, Lucy," said Anne. She looked at Sarah warily, but Sarah smiled at her so warmly that Anne lost her anxious look.

After Sarah, Tom, and Anne left, Lucy and Jeremy were alone together. They were silent for a little while. Then Jeremy said, "I've got something to ask you." He looked so serious that Lucy could not imagine what it might be.

"Will you come to the Clare College May ball with me?" he asked.

Lucy had not expected this. May balls were romantic affairs with lots of dancing and couples kissing in the moonlight—or so she had imagined them. She had never thought of Jeremy as anything but a good friend and could not think of dancing with him, let alone kissing him. He simply did not attract her at all. Oh, how she longed for Peter to appear and ask her the same question. She had not told anyone except Charlotte about Peter, nor had she confided in Jeremy. But Peter was in Vienna and she was here, and now she had to decide about Jeremy. Her hesitation was not lost on him, and he said, "Oh, do say yes—I think we'd have such a jolly time. We can get all dressed up and punt up to the college along the river. It will be such fun. I've never been to a May ball before, and I would love to take you."

He was looking into her eyes with intensity. Lucy couldn't bear to disappoint him. She had no other invitations after all, and she wanted to know what a May ball was like. So she took a deep breath and said, "All right, I'd love to come with you; thank you very much for asking me."

Then Jeremy took her hand and kissed it. "Thank you," he said, "thank you." He left her. She heard him whistling down the corridor. Lucy tried to take in what she had just done. It was only then that she thought about Anne. She knew that Anne really liked Jeremy, and yet he had asked Lucy to the ball. But since Lucy did not feel at all romantic toward Jeremy she felt she could not possibly be a threat to Anne. She was going to the ball with Jeremy in friendship, not in love, so she thought there was no harm in it. It never occurred to her to compare herself with Fiona. Anne must know that she did not have designs on Jeremy. But still she thought she would not mention the Clare College May ball to her.

That evening she and Anne walked down into Cambridge for the talk. Lucy asked, "How are things between you and Sarah now?"

"Well, I don't feel that she really is a true friend. Jeremy has helped me see that she just liked my being dependent on her and having my adoration. But now I think I can be fine on my own."

"So why are you coming to the talk?" asked Lucy

"Well, I'm very interested in the topic," said Anne, "so I thought I'd go anyway. Sarah probably doesn't care one way or the other. She came round only to invite you to go, and then she included me since I was there with Jeremy."

"I thought she was very pleased when you said you would come," said Lucy soothingly.

They had reached King's, where the talk was to be given, and found Sarah and Tom waiting outside the room. Inside there were only a few people. The talk was given by a small black man with a big voice. He told about the struggles of black men and women against the ruling Afrikaner government and its policy of apartheid. He told about the imprisonment of Nelson Mandela, leader of the African National Congress, and others who had also been tortured. He talked about the opposition to apartheid and the division between those who supported an armed struggle and those who preached non-violence. Lucy found herself taken out of her comfortable world in which she was free to do virtually whatever she liked into one of violence and strife in which men and women of principle were prepared to die for their beliefs in justice, and did. It made her own concerns seem petty. She came away with Anne feeling that she wanted to make something of her life—that she wanted to work for the good of others, not just for herself.

But as she walked home with Anne all she could think about was the May ball, not telling Anne about it, and her sense of guilt that maybe she should not have agreed to go with Jeremy. Suddenly Anne said, "I've invited Jeremy to the Oldwick May ball, and he's said yes. Do you think I did the right thing?" Lucy was so taken aback that she just laughed. It was so like Jeremy, hitting all the angles. "I think you did exactly the right thing," she said, "and I hope you have a wonderful time." All her worries about Anne disappeared; Jeremy was just very successfully playing the field.

The next week Lucy went shopping for an evening dress to wear at the ball. Charlotte went with her, as she was going to the Oldwick ball. "I really like Nigel," she said of the man she had invited. "He's tall and friendly, and he comes from a wealthy family! I'm just dying to see what a May ball is like."

"So am I," said Lucy.

They went into several shops and finally found a dress for Lucy. It was a beautiful light-blue taffeta dress with a very low neckline and a high waist. She thought it made her look like a woman from a Jane Austen novel. Charlotte declared that all the dresses were too expensive for her, led Lucy into a big department store, and bought a beautiful white nightgown. It looked just like a silk evening dress with thin straps and a low, lacy neck. Lucy was full of admiration, but Charlotte shrugged it off. "You just have to buy what you can afford," she said airily. "Come on, let's go and find some shoes."

This expedition put Lucy in the mood to have a lovely evening, not romantic, but fun. She didn't even think about what Jeremy's feelings toward her might be.

LLL

The evening came, the weather was beautiful, and Jeremy arrived wearing a dinner jacket and black bow tie. "He looks really nice," thought Lucy. "He's even washed his hair." He looked at Lucy admiringly. They both just said together, "You look wonderful," and laughed with excitement. Jeremy had rented a punt, and they went down to the river; Jeremy punted down to Clare. Many other couples were punting down the river all dressed up, laughing and talking. They tied up their punt, got out onto the grass—very carefully in Lucy's case—and went into the college to explore. The whole college was lit up. All the courts were floodlit. Tables and chairs had been set up where one could sit and drink wine in the open air. In the refectory there were fairy lights and a grand buffet set out on long tables. Two other very large rooms had been set up for dancing. In one of them a string quartet was playing waltzes, and in another a band was playing rock and roll, particularly the Beatles. Lucy longed for Peter when she heard the Strauss waltzes, but Jeremy led her firmly to the room with the band and proceeded to dance with her in a very expert fashion. Lucy was amazed.

"Where on earth did you learn to dance so well, Jeremy?" she asked.

"Oh, I learned in my teens, and now I'm a member of a dance club.

Our teacher once told me that women like men who can dance, so I took her seriously!"

He now led her into the other room where the string quartet was playing quicksteps and foxtrots. Lucy loved the dancing and was quite happy to be led around the room in Jeremy's arms.

They joined some friends from the orchestra for supper and sat outside together in the court. There was a lot of laughter as people told stories about their year in the orchestra.

"Wasn't it awful when old 'One-Two' made each desk play the most difficult part alone in front of the whole orchestra?" asked Lucy. "But I was lucky – I had Chris for my partner, and he's such a good cellist he can manage anything."

"Nonsense," said Chris, a stocky young man with a broad fine face, "you were great too."

"Well, I wasn't at all fine," said Jeremy, "but of course I had Hannah beside me." Hannah not being there, this remark passed without comment.

"Well, I loved it when we played 'Rite of Spring.' I learned so much about Stravinsky. All those insistent chords at the beginning, driving and driving, positively sexual," said Amanda, a violinist. There was shocked laughter at this; it simply wasn't done for women to refer to sexual things in public. Lucy looked sideways at Jeremy, who was laughing heartily. It had never occurred to her that music could be overtly sexual.

After supper, Jeremy said to Lucy, "Would you like to go for a walk outside? We could go down to the river and sit in the punt and smell the evening air." Lucy liked being with Jeremy and thought it would be nice to sit on the river and talk. So she said, "Let me just grab my cardigan and we can go."

The night was fine and clear; as they walked, Lucy could see the whole firmament. The moon was almost full and shone brightly. They sat in the punt under some dark trees. Jeremy put his arm round Lucy and she let him. He felt comfortable and warm. He didn't try to kiss her, for which she was grateful. Then, after a while, he turned to her and said, "Will you marry me, Lucy?"

At first Lucy could not grasp what he had just said to her. She turned to look at him. He was evidently completely in earnest. When she did not speak he said, "I'm so much in love with you. When I'm with you, I feel safe and happy. We get on so well together. Don't you think we'd make a good couple?"

"Oh, Jeremy," she said, "I love you too, but I can't marry you, I'm just not *in* love with you."

"But Lucy," he said, "You don't have to be in love with me for it to work. I have enough for us both. And you just said you do love me, so why can't we just get married and be happy always together?"

Lucy was overwhelmed with a flood of feelings and thoughts. As usual, her thoughts took over. She didn't want to marry anyone except Peter, but he certainly hadn't proposed to her, just that vague statement about the future. But she was his lover, and she felt totally committed to their love together. She couldn't imagine being happy making love with Jeremy and didn't know how to explain this to him without hurting him terribly. She remembered the moment that Adam had told her that he was going to marry Fiona—the feeling in the pit of her stomach as she took in this news, the feeling of total rejection. She couldn't do this to Jeremy. Yet she could never tell him about Peter. It would only make things worse for him. Then she thought of her father saying that Jeremy was "the salt of the earth," and she wondered how she could reject such a worthy suitor. As she thought of all these things, tears began to come, and she turned back to Jeremy and said, "It's no use, I can't love you the way you want me to, and I can't marry you. You just wouldn't be happy unless you had someone who was totally in love with you, and you deserve that. And the awful thing is that now we can't be friends any more, and I'll miss you terribly."

"Why not?" pleaded Jeremy, "why not?"

"Because it never works," said Lucy.

"How do you know?" said Jeremy.

"Well, everyone knows I was in love with Adam, and I found it very painful to be friends with him after he got engaged to Fiona; it was just awful. It made the pain go on much longer."

"But I'm not you," said Jeremy, "and I'm not going to go away. I don't want you to love me the way you loved Adam. You worshipped him as if he were a God—not a person at all—and he treated you callously while all the time accepting your love. I don't want that kind of love. It's sick. If you say you love me, then that's enough for me. But if you really don't want to be friends then we won't. It's up to you."

Lucy felt ashamed and guilty. She had either deeply underestimated him, or he was simply clinging to straws. Jeremy stood up precariously in the boat. "Come on," he said, "let's go back to the ball." She took his outstretched hand and they ran back across the lawn to the room with the band. It was playing a Beatles song with a slow beat. She suddenly thought of Danny. She had not seen him since before Christmas and wondered what he would make of her life now. It was but a passing thought. Jeremy took her in his arms, put his cheek against hers, and they danced together for a long time.

18

Hannah and Max

One summer day during the exam period Hannah and Lucy decided to play truant. They were both between exams and thought that nothing would be nicer than taking a punt on the river and punting up to Granchester. Hannah said, "Here, I'll punt first—you just sit and relax." So Lucy settled herself facing Hannah, who stood on the deck at the back of the boat expertly letting the pole drop into the water and pushing strongly so that the boat glided forward through the water. There was silence between them for a while as the banks with their overhanging trees slid past them. Then Hannah said suddenly, "I wish Max would ask me to marry him."

"Well," said Lucy after a moment, "I suppose that means that you love him a lot." Lucy did not use the words "in love" because she simply could not compare Hannah's relationship with Max to her own passionate feelings about Peter.

"Of course I do," said Hannah. "Everyone knows that, except possibly for Max."

"What do you mean?" asked Lucy.

"Well, we were talking the other day about our exams, and I was worrying that I would probably get only a 2-2 in the tripos, whereas Max is sure to get a first. Max said that he would do best in the paper on the New Testament because he knew it backward and forward and did not have doubts about his knowledge as opposed to his beliefs. And I thought, 'Oh no, here we go again with the doubts,' so I thought I would ask him if he had any doubts about me."

"Golly," said Lucy, "that was brave."

"He said I was the one person that he could really trust, that he would be only half a person without me, and that I made him very happy. I was thrilled by this confession and said he made me happy as well, and I thought we had a really good relationship. You know, Lucy, we just looked at each other and laughed, and it felt so right. And I was sure that he was going to ask me to marry him at that moment. But he didn't, and I just don't know what's holding him up."

"Maybe he's not ready to make a commitment to you while he's still working out the rest of his life," said Lucy, though even as she said it, she realized that it was not a very comforting thought. Hannah just looked thoughtful and went on punting away.

A few days later, to Lucy's surprise, the gnome put his head round her door and said, "Ah, I've found you at last, my love. May I come in?" Lucy jumped up and exclaimed, "Danny! What on earth are you doing here? How wonderful that you remembered which college I'm in."

"Well," he said, "Since chance has not brought us together in six months, I thought I'd better come and look you up." He looked around the room in a casual way and strolled to the window. "You're very nicely set up here," he said, "What a good view. Look at those gardens!"

"Yes," said Lucy, "they're looking particularly well at the moment, but they're lovely all year round. Would you like me to make some tea?"

"No, nothing," he said and sat down opposite her. "So how've you been, duckie?"

"Oh, I'm busy as always," said Lucy, "and I've got exams coming up, so I've been working really hard. What have you been doing?"

"Oh, managing away; but I've landed a job in London and I'll be moving there next month. It's in a film studio; just a menial job to start, but there's plenty of room to move up, so I'm chuffed."

"I'm so glad," said Lucy. She looked at him feeling at a loss for words. Then she said, all in a rush, "You know that friend of Anne's who Sarah said was interested in me? He just proposed to me, and I had no idea that he loved me so much."

Danny laughed. "So Sarah was right," he said. "What did you say to him?"

"I turned him down, even though I love him—just not in a passionate way. I said we couldn't possibly get married."

"Ah," said Danny, "so there are different kinds of love and only one kind for marriage?"

"Yes," said Lucy firmly. "Being in love is what counts. Have you ever been married?"

"No, but I would very much like to be. No luck there. Perhaps it's because I'm a funny-looking chap."

"Oh, Danny," cried Lucy, "you're not—you're wonderful, and you seem to know everything."

"No one ever knows enough," said Danny, suddenly serious. "It takes a long time to learn just one thing in life."

Lucy thought, "I know one thing in my life: I know Peter and I love each other, and nothing else matters."

Danny got up to leave. They exchanged their London addresses, and Danny said he would write when he got there. "Ta-ta, ducks," he said as he left. Lucy was sorry to see him go; he had become a true friend.

LLL

A week later, Hannah showed Lucy a mysterious message from Max. It read,

Dear Hannah,

Could you come to my rooms tomorrow, Tuesday, at two? I have something very important to tell you.

Love, Max

"I'm so excited," said Hannah, "though it's strange that Max would write to me instead of just coming right over to see me as he usually does. Maybe he's decided to propose and is just setting the scene, but I wonder why he's making me wait until tomorrow to find out. It's so unlike Max; he often does things on the spur of the moment and expects me to fit in. Remember that first kiss I told you about, Lucy, when he came bursting into my room with the mistletoe, quite determined to kiss me whether I wanted to or not? Perhaps he's going to buy me a ring and needs the time to do so."

Lucy listened to Hannah's flow of thoughts and felt distinctly worried. It all seemed eerily similar to the time Adam had invited her to come to his rooms on That Night to tell her about Fiona. But surely Max had no one else in his life besides Hannah. On the other hand, he had said he was going to tell her something, not ask her something. That also seemed a bit strange. He must be very sure what her answer would be. Well, of course he was sure; she had told him just last week that he made her very happy and they had laughed together. She said to Hannah, "Why don't you march right over to his rooms and ask him point blank what is going on?"

"Oh no," said Hannah, "I'd better wait until Tuesday; we always do things the way Max wants."

On Tuesday afternoon, Lucy was in her room studying for her last exam on the following day. It was Economic History, requiring the knowledge of facts as well as theory, and she was trying really hard to remember the dates of key inventions in the nineteenth century that had led to economic growth.

Suddenly, Hannah burst into her room with a white, distraught face.

"It's Max, oh God," she sobbed. "I can't bear it, I just can't bear it."

"What's happened to him?" cried Lucy. "Is he sick, has he been in an accident?"

Hannah threw herself on the bed and sobbed, great racking sobs. Lucy tried to put her arms around her but Hannah sat up and pushed Lucy away. "I'll tell you exactly what happened, and then you'll know how monstrous he is." She sniffed and then blew her nose.

"This afternoon, I cycled over to Max's rooms in Emmanuel, and when Max opened the door I saw he had a look of suppressed excitement on his face. He didn't kiss me but led me to a chair and said, 'I think you should sit down for this.' Then he started to walk around the room. He said he'd finally come to a life decision and that I should be the first to know, because I was the only one who really understood him. He said he knew I loved him and that I wouldn't stand in his way as his family would. I was really alarmed. It sounded all very independent and ominous. He hadn't gone down on one knee yet, and I thought maybe he was going on a trip round the world and wasn't planning to take me with him. He then flung himself into a chair and threw his arms back. 'I might as well just say it,' he said, looking at me: 'I've decided to become a monk. I'm going to go straight into a monastery after the end of term. I won't finish Cambridge. I've been talking to the monks at the monastery and they say they'll accept me as a novice whenever I like.'"

Lucy cried out, "A monk? What on earth did he mean?"

Hannah said, "You see—it's unbelievable, isn't it? I just looked at him and started to shake. I couldn't control it, so I hung on to the arms of my chair and said, 'So you mean, you're going to be a monk and we're not going to get married?' And Max just said, 'No, of course we can't get married. I've decided to give up everything, you and all my family and friends, and go to be with other people like me who are trying to find God, every single day. Then I'll lose my doubt. Remember we once talked about how Jesus calls us to give up everything and follow him? That's what I intend to do.'"

At this Lucy burst in, "This is all wrong, Hannah, why can't he go into the church and become a vicar? Then you could get married and he could have both, you and the church."

Hannah started crying again. "That's exactly what I said to him. And then I said, 'I thought you loved me. Last week you told me you were only half a person without me. Was that a lie?'" Now, with Lucy there, she was beginning to become angry. "And then you'll never believe what he said; he said he did love me, and I realized that it was the very first time he had actually said the words. And then he went on, 'But I can't preach to others with so much inner doubt. I just know that I want to be with God more than anything else in the world, and the way to do it is to become a monk.' By now I was furious and got even more angry when he had the nerve, the absolute nerve, to say he had hoped that I would support him in this and make his alb for him."

"My God," said Lucy, "I see why you're so angry," and indeed Hannah became silent for a while as she tried to calm her fury. Then more heaving sobs came from her. Finally she overcame her crying and said coldly, "I asked him whether he had any idea what this life decision, as he called it, was doing to me. And he seemed surprised at the question. 'Well, I knew it would be a shock,' he said, 'but I had hoped that since I know you love me you would understand.' He even looked pained and disappointed. So I said, 'You must have been thinking about this for ages; all those discussions with the monks and so on. Why didn't you tell me before now?'"

"This finally made him waver a bit. 'I just felt I had to be sure about what I was doing before I told you,' he said. What he meant was that he didn't want me to influence his decision, as if I would," said Hannah. "And then I suddenly realized that Max was actually enjoying this conversation. He was completely focused on himself and liked the feeling. His doubt and his faith seemed to be all bound up with himself, as if he could not separate his doubts about himself and his doubts about God. He was actually happy to be telling me how grand he had become to himself. So I said, 'Max, you must think me pretty stupid to have been assuming all along that we were going to get married, when the truth was that you were going to leave me forever.' And he had the nerve to say that he had got it wrong too, and that he thought I loved him more than I evidently did. You know, Lucy, the Max I loved isn't the Max who was talking to me then. He was so proud and convinced of his own rightness, and didn't care one jot for my pain. I'm so disillusioned; it's as if all our happiness this past year was based on a lie—as if it had never happened."

Lucy had been sitting quietly, not wanting to interrupt the flow of Hannah's misery although she could hardly bear it herself. She felt for Hannah deeply, but Hannah pushed her away every time she tried to hold her hand, so she sat in silence and concluded that just sitting there would be the most comforting thing she could do. Now Hannah stopped crying and said, "I told him I never wanted to see him again, but I hoped he would have a good life, and then I left."

Finally Lucy said, "Does Max understand how much he's hurt you?"

"No, doesn't seem to care. That's the worst part of it—he doesn't care what happens to me; he just cares what happens to him. It's monstrous." Hannah wiped her red eyes and blew her nose yet again.

Lucy said, "Would it help if I went to talk to him?"

"You can if you like," said Hannah "but he won't listen, you'll see, he's made up his mind. If he wanted to go into the church, why couldn't he just become a vicar? Then he could marry me and we could still be a couple. He's gone mad; you'll see he's just gone mad."

Lucy said, "You stay here and rest, and I'll go and see if he'll talk to me." She left Hannah crying again, got on her bike, and hurried over to Emmanuel. She was trying to make sense of the whole thing, but her immediate concern was for Hannah.

She found Max in his room sitting in a chair peacefully smoking his pipe. He had a benign expression on his face and showed no awareness of having just dropped a bombshell that would affect several lives so deeply.

He looked up when Lucy entered, read her face, and said, "I know why you've come. You'd better sit down."

"Oh Max," said Lucy, "I've just left Hannah and she's devastated. Are you really going to go through with this?"

"I suppose you mean by 'this' the most important decision of my life?" asked Max dryly.

Lucy said, "Hannah keeps crying 'Why is he doing this?,' and I need to know too."

"You can't believe I haven't thought about it thoroughly," stated Max, drawing on his pipe.

"I suppose you have," said Lucy, "but do you really understand how unhappy Hannah is?"

"I suppose she is," said Max. "I have thought and thought about it and it came down to a choice between marrying Hannah and finding God, and finding God is intrinsic to my being. Hannah wouldn't be happy if I was still in a state of doubt. Surely she'll get some comfort from knowing that I am happy. You've read *Interior Castle*, so you must know what it takes to find God. There's just no other way for me than to go into a monastery and devote my life to that quest. And part of that devotion is giving up Hannah."

"You make her sound like a human sacrifice," said Lucy angrily. "Why can't you see her as a real person who could help you rather than get in the way? Why can't you marry her and become a vicar?" She got up from her chair and started to pace the room—that room where they had had the lovely playing party. She looked out onto the court and saw some students laughing together. "How can anyone deliver so much pain?" she thought. Then she thought of Adam. He had already betrayed her in this room. He had caused her untold pain. She thought that Hannah and Max had found the secret to happiness. She was wrong.

"I can't preach to others when I am in doubt myself," said Max. "Can't you try to understand my point of view for once, or is it just a question of women always sticking together no matter what?"

"Well, what is your point of view?" asked Lucy.

"All my life I've loved God. Hannah knows that. The doubt that has seized me happened as soon as I began thinking of devoting my life to

God. I began to think that I was not worthy to be a monk—that you had to have a rock-solid faith before you could go into a monastery. But no one has a rock-solid faith. Do you? Don't you just try to live your life and hope that your faith will come? That's what you told me yourself, Lucy. Well that's what I want to do, but I want the best possible chance to find and live my faith always. I want to be open to God all the time, and I can do that only in a monastery with other people like me. So I thought about whether it would be fair to Hannah to marry her feeling as I do, and I concluded that it wouldn't. She deserves someone who can be happy with her." Max stopped speaking and looked at Lucy.

She still felt angry but now there was sadness too. "I just can't understand how you could have had such a long relationship with Hannah without letting her know your thoughts about this monk idea. It was so deceptive. How can you think of yourself as a Christian who loves others when you were playing with Hannah's love? Surely relationships with other people are what we're here for, aren't they? Loving God through loving others; isn't that what Jesus told us to do? I just don't see how you can completely give up other people—your mother and father, and Hannah who loves you so much. I think it's very sad for all of you."

"I'll miss Hannah more than she'll ever know," he said.

"Well, I hope you do," said Lucy.

"She says she doesn't want to see me again," said Max.

"Well, why should she? After what you've done, why should she?" asked Lucy. She kept trying to think of ways in which Max's decision could be reversed. But she knew it couldn't. Hannah had lost him, and that was all there was to it.

"Good-bye Max," she said, and left.

When Lucy got back to her room, Hannah was gone. Lucy thought she had better not pursue her. What Lucy had heard from Max was not going to help at all. Perhaps Hannah needed to be alone. Lucy went back to her revision and finally went down to dinner hoping to see Hannah. She was not there, but Anne was. She had just been to the Oldwick May Ball with Jeremy. "How did it go, Anne?" asked Lucy.

"Oh, we had a lovely time," said Anne "and just wished you had been there with us. Jeremy dances so well. Did you know this about him? Charlotte was there with a very nice chap called Nigel. She was wearing a fabulous white dress. Mine was very ordinary, I'm afraid." Lucy was glad to listen to this chatter from Anne and tried not to feel too guilty about what had happened between herself and Jeremy.

"Where's Hannah?" asked Anne. "I wanted to ask her how her last paper went."

"I don't know," said Lucy, "she's had a bit of a shock." It suddenly occurred to Lucy to worry about where Hannah was. She remembered how she had gone down to the river when Adam had told her about Fiona and thought about death. Could Hannah do the same thing? Surely she was much too sensible. Lucy got up quickly and ran to Hannah's room. Lucy knocked on the door. "Hannah," she said, "let me in; it's me, Lucy." There was no reply. "Please let me in, I'm worried about you," she said in a louder voice. Then she tried the door. It was locked. What on earth should she do now? How stupid she had been to leave Hannah alone with her grief. "Hannah," she said again, "if you don't open this door, I'm going to the Porter's lodge to ask them to unlock it for me."

At this, the door was pushed open, and Lucy flung herself into the room. Hannah was standing in her underwear holding a pair of scissors in her hand. There was blood on her wrists. She was crying. At first Lucy was so shocked she started to cry too. Then she grabbed the scissors from Hannah and threw them in the wastepaper basket. "What are you doing, Hannah?" she cried. She grabbed a towel and started to wrap Hannah's blood-soaked arms, all the while crying, "Why are you doing this, why, why?" But of course she knew. Hannah slumped down onto the bed, her arms hanging over the side. Lucy got the scissors out of the wastebasket and started to cut the towels into strips. Her hands were shaking. She bound the wounds as best she could and then went into the hall and shouted "Help, help!" No one. There was silence in the corridor. She couldn't bear to leave Hannah to find help, so she returned to her side and sat on the bed next to her. "Hannah," she said, "I can't leave you, so you have to get dressed and go with me to the Porters lodge, where they can call an ambulance. You can wear your coat so no one will see the towels. Thank God you let me in." Hannah just sobbed and took in her breath in great gasps, but she did not resist. Lucy put her arm round her, and together they hobbled out. Then things moved like lightning, and within a few minutes Hannah was in an ambulance speeding toward the hospital with a nurse on either side of her. Lucy was not allowed to go with her. Instead she was sent to see the moral tutor, Mrs. Johnson, to explain what had happened. Mrs. Johnson said she would go to the hospital to find out about Hannah's condition and then call her parents.

As Lucy walked back to her room she was at first very sad, and then she became angry. What Max had done was such a betrayal. But then she also thought of Hannah's trying to kill herself as a betrayal. She could have stayed in Lucy's room until Lucy had returned. But Lucy understood completely why she didn't; the pain was just too great to bear. She had not thought Hannah capable of such enormous feeling. She had consistently put Hannah in a box—safe and unflappable—and she was wrong again.

Hannah had completely misjudged how serious Max was about his faith and so had she, just as she had misjudged Adam's feelings toward her based on one kiss. And then she had also misjudged Jeremy's feelings toward her. When it came to love, she had got everything wrong, totally wrong. She felt deeply ashamed and humiliated. How could she have been so blind so often?

Back in her room, Lucy lay on her bed and thought and cried. Hannah's suicide attempt had shaken her to the core. She was dying to talk to someone who would understand. She immediately thought of Jeremy and decided she had to believe him when he said he wanted to be her friend. He was also Max and Hannah's friend, so he had to know sometime what had happened. She cycled over to his room but he was not in, so she left an oblique note and asked him to come and see her as soon as possible. Then she went back to her room and tried hopelessly to concentrate on her work.

A short time later, Jeremy appeared. She had not seen him since the May ball, so she greeted him rather anxiously. But when he put his arms around her and held her close, she started crying. "Max is going to be a monk, and Hannah cut herself," she sobbed into his shoulder. "Well, I knew about Max, but not about Hannah," said Jeremy. "Let's sit down and talk." They sat together on the bed, and Jeremy held Lucy's hand. "Max told me yesterday about his decision," said Jeremy, "and I said to him that it was his life after all, but it all sounded a bit extreme to me. Since I don't believe in God I find it hard to understand how anyone can be so intense about their belief. I suppose in his terms it makes some sense. But I never believed Hannah would be so stupid. I thought she was steadier than that."

"So did I; I just didn't realize how much she was in love with Max," said Lucy. "I've been wrong about so much. I feel such a fool."

"You've nothing to blame yourself for," said Jeremy. "You couldn't have known any of it. Love makes people go all peculiar."

"I know," said Lucy, "very."

In all this time Lucy had not once questioned her own love for Peter. Now a breath of thought crossed her mind that she might be wrong about Peter, just as she had been wrong about Adam. Danny had said that it takes a long time to learn things in life. But the thought passed, and Lucy was secure again. She and Peter would be always together.

Jeremy and Lucy sat together with their thoughts for a while. Finally Jeremy said, "You make some cocoa and get to bed and we'll see how things look tomorrow."

"I've got an exam at nine," said Lucy gloomily.

"I'll come over at 8:30 and take you there," said Jeremy. "Then we can have lunch somewhere afterward."

"Thank you," said Lucy, "thank you very much." He was being so kind in the face of her rejection of him that she could hardly understand it. But she accepted his kindness and was grateful for it.

Later the next day, having heard from Mrs. Johnson that Hannah would like to see her, Lucy went up to the hospital. Hannah was sitting in a chair in a sunny part of the sitting room. As soon as she saw Lucy she got up and gave her a hug. "I know I shouldn't have done it," she said, "I know he's not worth it. I was so angry I couldn't help it; I couldn't bear the pain."

"I know that pain," said Lucy, "and it is truly awful." In that moment she realized that her love for Peter had taken away the pain she had felt after Adam's rejection but not suppressed the memory. The odd, disheveled man who had watched her as she looked at the darkly flowing river came into her mind. Perhaps the memory would always be with her. She did not know how to comfort Hannah. Surely it couldn't be right for women to think about killing themselves for a man. How abject! Sarah must never know.

"Let's stick together," she said to Hannah. "We'll do this together."

Part IV

Summer

19

The End of Easter Term

The Easter term had ended, and everyone at Oldwick was preparing to go home and start their summer activities. Hannah was already at home with her family. Lucy had received a 2-1 in her first-year exams and was reasonably satisfied. Max got a first in his second-year exams, making Lucy feel even more strongly that it was a waste for him to leave Cambridge so soon. He came to say good-bye to her.

"Let's go for a walk," he said. They walked out into a sparkling summer day. Cambridge was full of people all celebrating the end of term. The punts were so numerous that the river was blocked behind King's. There was such a festive air that Lucy felt happy in spite of all that had happened. Peter was coming to England to visit her at home in London, and she hoped they would really be able to get to know each other better.

They found a bench beside the river, and Max asked, "Do you know how Hannah is? She won't write to me. I think her family has forbidden her from having any contact with me."

"That's perfectly understandable, don't you think?" said Lucy. "After what you did to her she will need time to recover." Lucy was still almost as angry with Max as Hannah had been. It had been unconscionable for Max to take all Hannah's love and not let her participate in making a decision that affected them both so profoundly. Max was cowardly and selfish.

Max did not acknowledge his responsibility toward Hannah at all. Instead he said, "Well, I just want you to know that I didn't expect that this would happen when I told her about my decision. I was shocked when I heard from Jeremy what she had done. I mean, I knew she would be disappointed, but I'd no idea she would try to hurt herself."

Max started to light his pipe as he said this, and Lucy saw that his hands were shaking.

Lucy softened slightly. "You're not alone, nobody thought she would cut herself," she said. "I think it was all just a terrible shock and that she was very angry."

"I can't change my mind, even though this has happened. I'm still going to become a monk."

"I know," said Lucy.

"I won't be able to see anybody for six months, but after that I hope you'll come and visit me," said Max.

"No, I don't think I will," said Lucy. "You are asking me only because you think you will want to find out about Hannah, and I'm certainly not going to tell you. It will be better for Hannah to have a clean break."

Max looked sad, but nodded his head. He was lost to the outside world. It seemed that they had said everything that was to be said, and they sat in silence for a while, watching the punts go by.

He walked her back to Oldwick, and said good-bye. It was the last she saw of him. Lucy thought a great deal about Hannah after this meeting with Max and waited each day for a letter from her.

A few days later Lucy began packing her things to go home. She was sad to say good-bye to her old room, the scene of so many important events in her life. She had been so sure about her love for Adam, and then so miserable when he had announced his engagement. But now she was sure that she loved Peter and she was determined that this time she would not make a mistake. She would try to see him clearly and build a solid relationship with him, one based not on infatuation but on mutual understanding. She believed that one week of love-making and music in Vienna was a foundation to build on.

As she was packing, Adam came in. She had last seen him with Fiona at the orchestra's end-of-term party, and they had exchanged a few words. He was impeccably dressed, as always, and looked cheerful. He kissed her cheek and said, "I hear you're going to see Peter this summer." Lucy blushed. She had not mentioned Peter to him at all; Peter must have told him about her.

"Yes," she said, "he's coming to visit me soon in London."

"Well, he's a fast worker," said Adam with an edge in his voice. Lucy was surprised that Adam seemed annoyed with her. After all, he had rejected her, rather than the other way round.

"What business is it of yours who I see?" she said.

"I just don't want to see you hurt," said Adam sitting down uninvited in a chair by the fireplace.

"Why should Peter hurt me?" She asked.

"Do you love him?" asked Adam.

"Yes, I do," said Lucy. "Why shouldn't I?"

"It's just so obvious," said Adam.

"What is?" asked Lucy.

"That you would fall in love with my brother."

"What is it to you?" asked Lucy. "You don't love me, so why should you care?"

"But I think you still love me," said Adam, looking at her seriously.

Lucy was surprised by the whole direction of the conversation. She had never said that she loved Adam in all their time together. She wanted to tell him just to leave the room. But instead she felt impelled to say, "No, I'm afraid I don't, not anymore. I did, but I've stopped. You can't just keep on loving someone if there's no return."

"But isn't that just when you met Peter? Didn't you just start loving him instead of me?" asked Adam.

Lucy found herself becoming angry. She said, "You're making me think that you care about me after all and that you're jealous of Peter. But that's too bad because the fact is that I don't love you at all anymore."

There was a hot silence between them. Adam looked at her with fury.

"Really?" he said.

"Please leave," said Lucy. She couldn't bear him any more. He got up to leave, but before he did he drew her to him rather forcefully and kissed her full on the lips. "Now do you say you don't love me?"

Lucy felt a coldness come over her. She was completely indifferent to him. The touch of his lips meant nothing to her. She was furious that he had taken such a liberty.

"If that was a test, then you failed it," she said. "Now will you please go?"

"I think you are not doing Peter any favors," he said as his parting shot.

Lucy flung herself on the bed and cried with fury. Adam's arrogance was beyond belief. How dare he kiss her in an attempt to show her that she still loved him, how dare he? He had no idea how she loved Peter, how different their relationship was from hers with Adam. She and Peter loved each other. She adored being with him; they talked about everything from music to religion to politics. How dare Adam think that she was just transferring her love from him to Peter after the wedding? She was now worried that Adam had told Peter that she had not stopped loving him despite his marriage to Fiona. She wondered how Peter's feelings about her had changed now that Adam had attempted to undermine their relationship. Well, she was not going to let this assault affect her relationship with Peter one bit. She would spend some time with him and explain everything. But still she cried with fury and bit the pillow. She wished she could tell Hannah what had happened; but she found herself once more alone and in tears. They were tears of anger, not sadness.

Later, she went downstairs to the last dinner in Hall. There she found Anne, and they sat together and munched on chicken and mashed potatoes for a while in silence. Finally Lucy asked, "What are you doing for the summer, Anne?" She hadn't seen Anne for several days. Anne looked very embarrassed and said looking down at her plate, "Jeremy and I are going on a holiday to Spain." Then she raised her eyes and looked at Lucy. "It may seem strange, going together, just the two of us. But we get on so well, and thought it would be fun. And you said you would be busy all summer. I hope you don't mind about this."

Lucy was very relieved but she didn't quite know what to say. So she ignored the question and all that it implied, and simply said, "Will you be taking all your camera equipment?"

"Of course,"' said Anne, clearly also relieved that Lucy had not reacted as if she disapproved. "We're going to start in the Pyrenees and end up at Gibraltar, and come home with what we hope will be some excellent photographs. Then we're both going to find jobs to pay for the whole thing. It's the wrong way round, I suppose, but you know after term one is dying for a change of scene. We'll send you lots of postcards."

"Yes, do," replied Lucy, "I'll be longing to hear from you." Then Anne said, looking at Lucy with a clear face, "I know he likes you better than me. I could see he did as soon as he met you. But now that you're so busy I think he and I can continue to be friends as we always were before he met you."

Lucy was quite humbled by Anne's openness and generosity. Anne did not seem to resent Lucy the way Lucy had so fiercely resented Fiona. She seemed able to accept Jeremy on his terms because she loved him. It was true that, despite her refusal, Lucy felt a pang that Jeremy was now going out with Anne. It was so comforting to have his love, his enthusiasm for her, his intelligent conversation, his expertise on the dance floor. He was a true friend on whom, up to now, she had been able to rely. And then he had been such a support over Hannah. But she did not feel that she had exploited him by accepting all this from him, and she did not feel she had lost everything to Anne. Jeremy was so different from Adam; she was confident she could continue to be friends with him as he had said he wanted the night of the May Ball. However, when she thought about how she had behaved toward Adam because he did not love her, she now felt ashamed. It wasn't Adam's fault that she had fallen so desperately in love with him, any more than it was her fault that Jeremy loved her. The unbearable thought came to her that maybe Adam was right and that she was punishing him by loving Peter. She pushed this thought away and looked back at Anne. "I just hope you both have a wonderful time in Spain," she said. They left the dinner table and walked together slowly upstairs.

20

Sarah and Tom

The next day, Sarah and Lucy were doing their washing. There were two large tubs in the laundry room for the washing of personal items; bed linen was sent out. Sarah was washing her denim suit. "It's my interview suit, which I never wear now," she explained to Lucy. "I thought I might try and sell it to someone to earn a little money; then I'll be able to afford to buy a copy of *Piers Plowman* I've seen in the secondhand bookshop." Lucy laughed. "No, really," said Sarah, not at all offended. "After the suit has dried, I'll do my best at ironing the thing and then see if I can get a good price for it. I hate having no money to spend on luxuries. I know you're always craving the steak at the Turk's Head Grill and never having enough money for it, but I crave books."

"I know," said Lucy. "Come on, let's hang up our stuff and I'll come with you to your room and help you pack while we talk."

"Did I tell you," said Sarah as they contemplated the mess in her room, "that next year I've decided to live out of college?"

"Why on earth would you want to do that?" asked Lucy. "I think being in college is the most wonderful thing in the world."

"Well, it will be my third year," replied Sarah, "and I feel like having more freedom. I've found a flat on Harvey Road that I can share with Charlotte. It's at the top of an old Victorian house. The street is very quiet and ends at Fenners, the cricket ground. From the garden of the house you can actually hear the crack of the bat against the ball and the scattered claps and cheers that go up after a good hit. I think this will be a soothing accompaniment to my reading."

"The way you describe it makes it sound fantastic," said Lucy, impressed.

"But now I'm going home and have to find myself something to do in the summer vacation," said Sarah. Lucy contemplated this problem as she folded a few sweaters and put them in a pile for Sarah to pack. Finding a summer job was a perennial difficulty for students; temporary jobs were hard to find.

"I suppose I could volunteer as you do in a secondhand bookshop," said Sarah, "but then I would still be beholden to my parents for support. Most political activities stop during the summer, and I really don't want to spend the entire summer at home."

"I know how you feel," said Lucy thoughtfully. Lucy did not want to own up to her own summer plans as she had not told Sarah about Peter. To tell the truth, she was embarrassed to do so. Sarah knew about her disappointment over Adam; Lucy felt Sarah had not been very sorry for her and thought that Lucy was well rid of him. Now, to confess her love for his brother seemed to invite ridicule. She did not know how she could explain to Sarah that this new love was different; this love was real and shared; this love was forever. Lucy had arranged for Peter to spend two weeks with her and her family in London, and then later she might join him again in Vienna. Even thinking about these plans made her feel that her relationship with Peter was solid. But she just said, "Well, we seem to have made a dent in the packing, so I'll leave you to do the rest. I've got to go and say good-bye to my tutor. I'll see you later."

Toward lunchtime Lucy was walking back into the college when she bumped into Sarah coming out. Lucy hardly recognized her at first, she looked so beautiful. Gone were the long skirt, the scruffy blouse scarcely tucked in, and the old cardigan. Gone was the red scarf around her head. Instead, Sarah was wearing a sky-blue full skirt and a crisp blue-and-white flowered shirt neatly tucked in at the waist. The weather was warm, so there was no need for a cardigan. Her hair was freshly washed and hung in lush curls over her shoulders. Only the clogs were the same. She looked beautiful, and the expression on her face was of open happiness. Lucy could hardly believe the transformation; she said, "Sarah, you look gorgeous, where are you off to?" Sarah looked sheepish, but she smiled her radiant pixie smile and replied, "Oh, nowhere in particular; I mean I'm only going to meet Tom for lunch at the Perch. It's such a nice day and we're going to sit out on the benches by the river. I'll see you later." She hopped on her bike and was gone in a flash. To Lucy, the idea of Sarah going out with a man was extraordinary, and that she should dress up for the occasion! Lucy couldn't wait to find out from Sarah how she got on.

A few hours later Sarah flung herself into Lucy's room. "Oh, I'm so excited I could burst," she said. "I'm going to spend four weeks in America with Tom." Her face was flushed and radiant with happiness, and she looked at Lucy with an expression that almost pleaded to be understood. Lucy said innocently, "You mean you're going to America with a man?"

"Oh, I know what you're thinking," said Sarah. "It's true. Up to now I've haven't found a man I could like and respect. I don't even like your friends, Lucy; I mean, Adam is so arrogant and Jeremy is sarcastic, and Max—well, what is there to say about him except that he comes across as rather full of himself—but Tom is so different." She paused and then, realizing what she had just said, looked at Lucy in a horrified way. "Oh Lucy," she said, "I'm so sorry; I didn't mean to insult your friends like that."

Lucy had blanched slightly under Sarah's onslaught. She was hurt by what Sarah had said but had to admit that she was near the mark in her descriptions. Her love for Adam had indeed blinded her to his arrogance; she knew Jeremy could be sarcastic, but he never was to her now that they had such a close friendship; and it was quite true that Max thought only about himself. So she said in a conciliatory way, "Oh, never mind about that, just tell me what happened between you and Tom, and why Tom is so different."

"Well, we met at the Perch and Tom was waiting for me on a bench outside. We sat there together for a while and looked at the river; you could smell the cut grass and the roses, and it was altogether lovely. Tom said I looked beautiful and not at all like the American girls who were always so smartly dressed and made up. And he said they always carry their books under their arm, no matter how many they have, and somehow dangle a tiny, wee handbag from one finger. Isn't that strange? All I've got is a large leather bag that holds everything, and I can put it on the back of my bike with no trouble, and Tom was highly approving. He said I was 'refreshingly different.' Then he went off to get us some beer and came back with a bag of crisps as well, which he called chips. The pub was really full and everyone was outside, and it was all very jolly. Then he took a sip of his beer and suddenly asked me if I hated men. I was so taken aback I hardly knew what to say, so I asked him what made him think that. He said, 'Well you've told me that you hate the patriarchy and that you think women are oppressed by men, and you think the institution of marriage is designed for the subjugation of women. Do you see me as a man who oppresses women?'"

Lucy laughed, "Well he's certainly understood all your views, hasn't he Sarah? I remember those meetings of the Circle when you tried to persuade us of all those things. So what did you say?"

"Well, I was actually a bit put out by the question," Sarah acknowledged, "so I just told him that I did not know him very well and asked him whether he was a man who oppresses women. I mean, why should I suddenly give up all my beliefs to please a good-looking man who is challenging them?"

"Good for you, Sarah," cried Lucy. "What was his response?"

"Well, of course he denied that he oppressed women and said that there are plenty of men who see women as equal partners and who want to work for justice for all downtrodden people, male or female. Then he said that both sexes need the other to love and to have children.

"I had to concede," said Sarah, "that we do need each other to procreate, but that then raises the question about who looks after the children. I told him we've had so many discussions about this in the Circle, and no one has found the answer yet. And certainly no one knows what to do with the sick child—who stays at home to look after it? And I couldn't believe that I was going over all this ground with a man. Then he asked me if I wanted to have children, and I said certainly not at the moment."

"He seems to have been asking you an awful lot of loaded questions," said Lucy. "How did things go from there?"

"I just told him all the things I love about my life as it is now. I love my independence, I love being away from home and waking up each morning knowing that I have only myself to please as I decide what the day is going to be like. Of course I go to my lectures and supervisions, and I spend lots of time writing my essays each week, but that's because I love being a student and want to do well. And then I love politics and want to be a politician some day and work for women's causes. But I don't see how marriage and a family fit in here."

Sarah paused, slightly breathless from the passion with which she had spoken. "You see, Lucy," she said, "I never really looked at my life before Tom encouraged me, and I am surprised how happy I am with it. Then Tom said that I had used the word love about six times, but never in reference to people! And then he asked me whom I love. I was really shocked and I couldn't tell whether he was referring to people in general or to himself. But since he asked I felt I had to respond to show that I wasn't the cold-hearted person he seemed to imply I was. So I said I loved my parents; well, everyone loves their parents. And I like my friends; you know I like you, Lucy, or I wouldn't be telling you all this. But I've never loved a man because I haven't found one that I even liked. Then Tom looked very pleased and said almost triumphantly, 'Oh good, then you're available.'

'What do you mean available?' I asked.

'I mean you're available to love me—if you feel like it,' he said. I felt he had put me in a false position so I said, 'Why on earth would I love you?' And he was looking at me in a very loving way and actually put his hand on mine and said, 'What I really mean is that I would like it very much if you did love me. I think you are a wonderful girl and you must know that I love you a lot.'"

"Oh Sarah," cried Lucy, "what a declaration!"

"Well it was," said Sarah, "But I had such mixed feelings and felt both happy and offended at the same time. I mean it was almost as if he was manipulating me with all that talk of love. So I said, 'I don't know how you can love me; we've only just met.' But Tom just got firmer and said he did love me and he thought I was the most interesting girl he had ever met. Then he softened a bit and said I didn't have to love him as long as I liked him a bit. And you know Lucy, I do like him a lot. He's the only man I've ever been interested in, and I don't feel he really wants to oppress me at all. But he was going far too fast for me, so I said, 'Let's have lunch and we can talk about this later.' I felt quite relieved when he took himself off to order the lunch and I had a chance to think a bit. When he returned and the lunch finally arrived, we just sat together watching the moorhens and swans swimming on the river and eating the weeds along the bank—I do love those birds! Suddenly he said he was going home to Atlanta for part of the summer and then back to Harvard to finish his research; wouldn't I like to go to Atlanta with him and meet his family? Then we could travel around a bit and see the South. Now you know, Lucy, that I'm dying to see America and see how American women are overcoming their barriers, and I'd even like to sit in on a consciousness-raising group. I've just read Betty Friedan's *The Feminine Mystique* from cover to cover. It's an amazing book. I wish we could resurrect the Circle just to discuss it. So you can imagine that Tom's suggestion was hugely seductive. I told him I'd love to go but I couldn't possibly afford it. But he had an answer for that too: He said if I would take him home with me to meet my parents he would persuade them to pay my fare, and after that I could stay with his family. So it wouldn't be too expensive. Everything became very clear to me then, and I said he could come to York and talk to my parents. He said, 'This is going to be just wonderful,' and I had to agree. Then he held my hand again and walked me back to Oldwick. Here I am, and my life has changed, and I can't believe it!"

Lucy got up and gave Sarah a hug. Sarah did not push her away. "I'm so happy for you," Lucy said. "I suppose you must really like Tom after all. And what an opportunity! America sounds so different from England; no wonder you're dying to see it."

In fact, Lucy was amazed that Sarah and Tom could make plans to be together for such a long time based on such a short acquaintance. And they hadn't even kissed! It didn't occur to her to think that her own relationship with Peter had developed even more suddenly. She wondered whether Sarah regarded Tom as she did Jeremy, as just a very good friend, or whether Sarah harbored secret romantic feelings about him that she was just not prepared to admit. In any case, for Sarah to be excited about a man was the cause for endless rumination.

21

Peter

It was July, and at home in London Lucy was preparing for Peter's visit. Her parents were ready to receive him, though her mother told her she hoped that it did not turn out to be a matter of an engagement. "You're far too young, Lucy," she said one day as they were doing the washing up together. "You've still got two years left at Cambridge, and you must finish them." Mr. Page was his usual laconic self, but at least he didn't mention to Lucy that Austria was a landlocked country any more. No one talked about the fact that Peter was Adam's brother, and Lucy certainly did not bring up the topic. When she looked back on her unrequited passion for Adam she could hardly believe that she was the same person. How could she have been so deluded? She worried very much about what Adam might have told Peter about her. So far Peter had hardly mentioned Adam to her, and she decided that she was simply going to avoid discussing him. Adam was now irrelevant to her, and if thoughts of Ely occasionally came to her mind, she tried to focus on the feeling of spiritual awakening and nothing else.

Lucy left her house and walked to the station. She had given Peter instructions how to come, but still it was almost miraculous when she saw him alight and come toward her with his arms open. They hugged for a while and then walked back up the hill to the house, talking all the time. Peter was introduced to Mr. and Mrs. Page and to Anthea, who had just come down from Oxford. There they were, five people talking about the weather and the journey from Austria and what Lucy and Peter were planning to do during his two-week stay. Lucy couldn't believe it. Her fantasy world had finally intersected with her real life at home.

During the next week, Lucy and Peter walked on air together through London. They saw three plays; one opera, *La Traviata*; and went to museums, soaking themselves in art. They went back to Leicester Square to see if they could find the phone booth where they had first kissed, but they couldn't agree which one it was. Lucy was always eager to hear about Peter's family and life in Austria. But the one subject they did not talk about during the entire stay was their future together. Lucy's happiness was so overwhelming that she did not look further than the next moment. One evening, they sat in the living room together listening to Mozart's clarinet quintet on the radio. Lucy lay down on the sofa and put her head in Peter's lap. He stroked her hair and her face. She felt they were completely at ease with each other. "This is bliss," she thought. "I'll never want anything in my life ever again except for this. I am totally and completely happy."

One day they took the train to Cambridge, had coffee at the Copper Kettle, and then began a great tour of the town. It took them so long to admire King's, Clare, and Trinity that it was late in the afternoon when they finally arrived at Oldwick. "This is my home from home," said Lucy proudly as they walked through the sunken gardens and admired the vast red-brick buildings. "I have been happy here, but especially last term when I had your letters to read every week." She omitted to mention the long misery she had endured after Adam's engagement, which had lasted until she met Peter. As they sat together on the train back to London, Peter said, "Do you truly love me, Lucy?" Lucy wished he had just told her of his own love, but she replied, "Yes, with all my heart," and kissed him.

On their final day they walked into Greenwich park where there was a little café and sat down together with their coffee. They had a piece of undistinguished cake between them and laughed at how they really wanted Apfelstrudel with whipped cream. Lucy looked expectantly at Peter, who was looking at her with his twinkling eyes.

He said, "Why are you looking at me so seriously?"

She did not reply at first, but then said all in a rush, as if to get the words out before she could stop herself, "I think we ought to decide a few things between us."

Peter asked quietly, "What things?"

Lucy said, "I just want to know if what we have together is real. Sometimes I think you really love me as much as I love you, but then sometimes I wonder if that's true."

There was a long silence. Finally Peter said, "But weren't you in love with my brother?"

Lucy was stunned. The worst had happened as she feared; Adam had indeed told Peter everything. She was speechless for a while. Then she said, "Oh, I see." Peter said nothing; he just looked at her sadly. There was more silence. The cake lay untouched on the plate. Then Lucy said, "Of course, he would tell you wouldn't he? That's the first thing he would do when he found out you liked me. How stupid of me, how totally stupid."

She paused, then she said, "But that's not important to us, it's just not relevant."

Peter said, "I think it is."

Lucy was desperate. "Look," she said, "you've loved others before you met me. I never assumed you didn't. So why does this matter? Besides, you are the one I love. The thing with Adam was an infatuation. He never loved me the way you do, and I never loved him as I love you. Mozart loved two sisters; it's not so strange."

Peter sipped his coffee slowly, put down his cup firmly and said, "But maybe you love me because you want to revenge yourself on Adam. How can I trust you when you say you love me? All my life Adam has come first. And now it turns out that the person I thought I could really depend on has been Adam's lover. He has come first again."

Lucy said passionately, "We were never lovers. It was a disaster from the start. All Adam wants to do is to control and dominate women. He's not interested in love. Besides, he wanted Fiona at the same time. She's his slave. She does everything for him and he likes it. He needs to be constantly worshipped. You're so different from him. You're wonderful and open, and I thought you wanted to share everything with me."

With this speech Lucy completely betrayed her former self, her experience at Ely, and all she had suffered on Adam's behalf. Peter said, "That's just the point. With you I knew I could have a real partner. But...." His voice trailed off. Lucy was still on the attack, and she said, "Oh, so you're saying that you don't want a real partner? That you're just like Adam?"

Peter asked, "Why didn't you tell me about Adam at the very beginning?"

Lucy felt she had her whole future to defend. She replied, "What would have been the point? I didn't love him any more. I saw him for who he is, and I didn't love him. And he never loved me, so what was there to tell?"

Peter said, "I still think you want revenge and you're using me to get it."

Lucy felt she was in a quagmire, struggling and struggling to get out. Against her will she became more and more dishonest. "It's true," she said. "At first I did feel angry toward Adam. He used me and he led me on all the time he was seeing Fiona. But when I found out where things stood, my love for him just dried up and I was left with no feeling at all about him."

The funny thing was that at no point had she felt angry toward Adam except for the very last time he had come to see her. She had felt only love and grief. Everything she was telling Peter was a lie. Peter was relentless.

"Then why did you go to the wedding?" he asked.

"I don't know, I don't know," she cried. "I suppose I was under the illusion that we could all still be friends as they both told me. They said we should be friends. Or perhaps . . ." she said, clutching at the truth in a last-ditch attempt to save herself, "perhaps I just wanted to see the bloody deed done."

"Then you do still love him after all." Peter's vise slammed shut, and she was caught.

"No, I don't, I don't," she protested ever more feebly. "Why are you cross-questioning me like this? Adam is not the point. What matters is what's going to happen to you and me. You're the one I love, not Adam."

The shadows of the afternoon were lengthening. Lucy felt that time was running out. Peter said, "I believe that you think you love me. But I'll never know whether you really do. Adam will always be between us. I don't think we can go on." What Lucy feared the most had been spoken.

She fought on, "But that's just what Adam wants," she said. "He's jealous of you and wants to spoil things. He can't bear it that I should love anyone after him, least of all his own brother. He's just a jealous spoiler. Can't you see that?"

Peter said, "Look, we're talking about my brother. I love him, and I don't think he is as bad as you make him out to be. He told me you loved him, and you have now told me you loved him, that's a fact." Peter looked grim as he said this.

Lucy said, "But love is not a fact, it's a relationship, and I never had a real relationship with Adam. It was all one way. I did the worshipping and he did the taking."

Peter was still as relentless as ever. He said, "Oh, so you worshipped him?"

"Well, of course I did," replied Lucy. "Adam requires that of women. I was naïve. Falling in love is like a sickness that you catch. And you have some feverish symptoms, and then you get better and you don't feel the love any more."

"But you say you're in love with me; is that a sickness?"

"Of course not; don't you see that? Have you forgotten the Shostakovich concert when I felt my soul pouring into yours and knew that we could truly be together?" Lucy had at last reached her truth, and she looked pleadingly at Peter to see if he understood. But instead he said, "All we are doing is talking about your feelings. What about mine?"

"Oh," cried Lucy, "that's not fair. Of course I want to know your feelings. You just won't tell me what they are. What are they? Are you full of anger toward me?" She waited with fear for his answer. She felt all her happiness hung by a tiny thread.

At last Peter said, "No, not so much. It's just that I think all happiness has to be paid for with suffering. We were very happy at the beginning. But now this thing with Adam.... Now comes the suffering. It's what seems to be true about my life. I can never avoid the suffering." He sounded so sad that Lucy took his hand and said, "I don't know whether pain always comes after love. I don't want to believe it, but I suppose that if you are often disappointed then you begin to think that it always happens. But it doesn't have to happen to us. I know we can be happy together."

Peter said, "But it has already happened to us; the pain is here now." And at that moment Lucy knew she had lost him. She knew she could never convince Peter that he was now first in her eyes. The ghost of Adam would always be there between them.

She stood up and said in a trembling voice, "I think we'd better go home now. You need to pack for your train tomorrow. Peter did not contradict her. He just said, "Whatever happens to us, we will always be close in our hearts."

Lucy said, "So this is really good-bye?"

"It has to be, you know it does," replied Peter.

Lucy, said, "Yes, I know."

They fell into each other's arms and embraced for a long time. When she kissed him good-bye at the station the next day, she knew that, despite the enduring closeness he had promised, they would never see each other again.

Coda

During the summer Lucy mourned her lost love. She felt very sad but did not feel she had completely lost herself as she had felt with Adam. At first she thought to herself that Peter was a coward for letting her relationship with Adam destroy theirs together. He had put his hurt pride before their love; he had been fearful of committing himself to her. But then she thought about her own part in their relationship. She had deceived him from the beginning. It was out of fear that she would lose him if he knew about Adam that she had withheld the truth. She was just as much to blame as Peter for the way things had ended. Sometimes she railed at Adam in her heart for having twice spoiled a relationship. But then she would catch herself and realize that her relationship with Adam had been very much in her own mind and not based on mutual feelings. She was even prepared to consider the idea that she had fallen in love with Peter on the rebound. But she still thought that she and Peter had had something different together, and she really believed he had loved her for a while as much as she loved him. She had stumbled on the mystery of all human relationships—how to understand another person's feelings—and she felt she had let herself down. Maybe Peter was right when he said that all happiness must be paid for with suffering. However, with her inner optimism, she rejected this idea. She thought that love, though risky, could still bring happiness, and she was determined to keep looking for it. She still had two years left at Cambridge and would be more pragmatic in the future.

As the summer wore on she received letters from all her friends. Hannah wrote:

> *Dear Lucy,*
>
> *I just want you to know that I am feeling much better and am very grateful to you for helping me during that terrible time. My parents have been wonderful. I go to the hospital twice a week to see a psychiatrist there, and he has been very helpful. He has helped me see that Max is not a villain for doing what he really wanted to do, just very selfish, especially toward me. I never saw that side of him until the end. It always seemed to me that we were equals in our relationship, but of course we weren't. I just always did what Max wanted. I appreciate so much more now what Sarah was always preaching to us. It's hard to think independently when you are in love. It's true that love is blind.*

We are all going off to Scotland next week to do some walking. Then, when I come back, I'm going to start doing some real work in preparation for next term. Sarah says she is going to live in Harvey Road with Charlotte. I think I may join them in their flat. It will be good to step out.

I hope you're having a good summer. You did not say what you were going to be doing.But I hope it is interesting and fun. I'm so looking forward to seeing you again next term.

Lots of love from Hannah

Lucy was relieved to receive this letter. She hoped very much that Hannah would continue to be her friend. She knew that sometimes, when someone had been through a crisis, they didn't want to be with the people that helped them because they were a constant reminder of the humiliation. But Hannah did not seem as if she was one of these. Lucy hoped that, on the contrary, their relationship would be stronger. She had much more in common with Hannah now. They had both loved and lost, though even now she thought that she and Peter could have been together if only. . . . But what was the point of going over the same old ground? At least she felt she could now confide in Hannah. That was a great comfort.

Several postcards came from Jeremy and Anne, who were making their way across Spain. One read:

Dear Lucy,

We are thinking of you. Spain is glorious, the people, the food, the pace of life are all so humane. We love eating our dinner at ten o'clock. We are taking hundreds of pictures. It will take days to show you them all. Hope everything is all right with you.

Love, J. and A.

Lucy wondered whether her friendship with Jeremy and Anne would survive the new closeness between them. Perhaps she would simply be a fly in the ointment. Sometimes she thought of Jeremy's proposal and wondered if she should not have taken her father's advice. She had her feet on the ground when she was with Jeremy. She did hope she had not lost him altogether.

Charlotte, who was on holiday with Nigel in Paris, wrote:

Dear Lucy,

I was so sorry to hear that you are not going to see Peter any more. Frankly I think it's best to stick with the English; they are steadier and more honest. Nigel and I are getting on so well I sometimes can't quite believe it. Of course Paris is wonderful. We have been three times to see the Sainte Chapelle, it is so lovely. It reminds me of King's, although of course it is so much smaller. The rest of the time we spend in the Louvre and in cafes drinking coffee and eating pastries. I hope you will get over the Austrians soon. They're not worth too much mourning. Looking forward so much to seeing you next term.

Love, Charlotte

Charlotte's words were bracing to Lucy. She was mourning deeply and at first resented Charlotte's casual dismissal of all her pain. But she acknowledged that Charlotte's perspective was not altogether wrong, though she didn't agree that Englishmen were best; so many of them were buttoned up and unemotional. On the other hand, there was the example of Jeremy, who had been so kind and sensitive toward her in spite of his sarcastic way. She took comfort from the idea that there was life after Adam and Peter.

A week after Peter had left she received two lines from him:

> *Darling Lucy,*
>
> *I will never forget the wonderful times I spent with you in Vienna and London. You will always be in my heart.*
>
> *From Peter*

Lucy cried and cried when she read this. Why, oh why, couldn't he have trusted her that she really loved him? She had gone over and over in her mind the course of their relationship. She thought she would have loved him truly even if she had never known Adam. Later that summer, when she thought about the whole year more deeply, she realized that she was changed. She still had something from each brother that she could keep and hold onto. After all, it was Adam who had taken her spiritual feelings seriously and had introduced her to *Interior Castle*. She had been strengthened by this, and her search for God had become more real to her. This was a great gift. Then, Peter had taken her whole self seriously, body and soul. Their love-making had changed her into a woman and, in spite of his ultimate rejection, she was grateful to him. Peter had things the wrong way round. Suffering could make you stronger if you allowed yourself to see beyond it to the love that was real, even if it did not last.

So now it was over with both brothers, and she was left alone. When she confided this to her mother, she said firmly, "But you are not alone. You have your family and your many friends who love you and write to you constantly. There is more to life than being in love. You must do your work and do something for other people." Lucy remembered how she had felt after the talk about South Africa: how she had been moved by the plight of the suffering colored people under apartheid, and how she had thought that she should do something to help them. She also thought ruefully how quickly she had been distracted from these plans. Her mother was right, together with Chekhov. In work for herself and others lay her salvation.

The very next day she was about to leave for the bookshop when a letter arrived from Sarah:

> *Dear Lucy,*
>
> *I am in Atlanta with Tom. America is wonderful – so different from England you can't believe it. Everything here is enormous: the cars, the houses, the roads, the tomatoes, and the men – so tall and muscular. The countryside*

is beautiful and it is very, very hot. Tom's family has given me a welcome fit for a queen and everyone loves my accent. I think I am in love with Tom. You were right all along.

Love is wonderful, Sarah

This was the final irony. Even Sarah had now deserted her. Lucy tried to keep her spirits up and was preparing to go back to Cambridge when she received the following note:

Dear Lucy,

Meet me at the Cutty Sark pub in Greenwich on Saturday at 12:30 p.m. Just come!

Yours, Danny

There was no one she would rather see.

On Saturday she walked across Greenwich Park and down to the river. The old pub overlooked the water. She spotted Danny sitting on a bench looking at the river traffic, and hailed him. He jumped up, came over to her, and took her arm. "Come and have a beer and some lunch," he said. She followed him into the pub, where they found a table near the window. She was so pleased to see him, but somehow she could not find anything more to say except, "Thank you," until they were sitting with their lunch in front of them looking at each other. Danny said, "You're looking a bit sad; how've you been?" Lucy told him everything. She cried for Adam, she cried for Peter, and she cried for herself; it was a great relief. "And now," she said, mopping her face, "I just don't know what to believe any more, about love, I mean. I don't seem to be very good at it." She took a drink of beer and felt it run down her throat. Danny looked out of the window. A tourist boat had just left the pier and was turning to make its way up-river to Westminster. Lucy followed his gaze and saw the tourists standing at the rail of the boat observing the view of Greenwich Palace and the park beyond. "There are so many people in the world," she said, "and yet I feel quite alone."

"You are not alone," said Danny, "you are with yourself."

"I don't feel I have much of a self at the moment," she replied.

"It's just that you've lost track of it," said Danny. "You'll find it, you just have to be patient and tolerate the waiting."

"But what about love?"

She raised her eyes to meet his, and felt his warm energy coming toward her. His face looked beautiful.

"Oh that," said Danny. Everything you've told me shows that you have a gift for love; you just haven't found the right connection yet. But you will; you will."

"Yes," she thought as she looked at him steadily, "I will."

18206472R00087

Made in the USA
Charleston, SC
22 March 2013